FEB 1998

The

UNCIVIL WAR

The
UNCIVIL WAR

Sheila Solomon Klass

Holiday House/New York

Library of Congress Cataloging-in-Publication Data
Klass, Sheila Solomon.
The uncivil war / by Sheila Solomon Klass. — 1st ed.
p.   cm.
Summary: Even with her father as principal, Asa Andersen is certain that
sixth grade will be perfect, until a new boy in school starts making fun of
her name and the baby her mother is expecting is born prematurely.
ISBN 0-8234-1329-2 (trade)
[1. Parent and child—Fiction.   2. Schools—Fiction.   3. Names,
Personal—Fiction.   4. Friendship—Fiction.]   I. Title.
PZ7.K67814Un   1997   95-15548   CIP   AC
[Fic]—DC20

For Mort—
friend, critic, husband,
for forty-four years.

S.S.K.

TM

Contents

The
UNCIVIL WAR

Dear Ann Landers,

I am twelve years old and I have a terrible problem. My mother loves me so much she is smothering me. I am way overweight because she stuffs me. I try to say no but she's such a good cook and I love to eat, so I end up eating it all.

Please help me.

Sincerely,
The Pudgeball
(a.k.a. Asa A. Andersen)

P.S. I wrote this letter a dozen times before, but I couldn't bring myself to mail it because even if you don't print my name Mom might read your column and guess it was me, and that would hurt her too much. I'm desperate.

Help!

1

The Pudgeball

I'd been antsy ever since we returned from church, waiting to get my mother alone. No luck. Like, my father was glued in his armchair all afternoon reading his *Times*. (I'm not allowed to start sentences with like, but I can *think* them.)

Finally, after dinner, when Mom was putting fresh water in her flower vase, Dad got up, kissed her on the cheek and said, "I guess I better begonia." (He's addicted to puns.)

We groaned, and he disappeared into his study. He was getting ready for the Elementary School Principals' Convention in San Francisco.

I held back, my pulse pounding in my ears—this time I would convince her—till I heard the door close.

"Mom, I need to talk to you about something important."

"Yes, dear?"

"I'm too fat. I have to go on a diet."

She smiled. "Asa, how many times have we had this conversation? You're a beautiful girl." She meant it, too. To her big was pretty, bigger was beautiful, and huge was gorgeous. When it came to me.

"I'm built like a hippo."

She laughed. "Don't be silly. You're sturdy-looking, not fat. You'll lose it all when you get older. Your skin and your coloring and your hair are all lovely. Everyone says you're a stunning girl."

"Mom, I'm the stunningly heaviest girl in my class."

She got that *mother* look of saintly patience in her eyes. "We live in a society that thinks emaciated is beautiful. But you and I come from another culture. Our genes are the genes of big people."

"Yours and Dad's maybe." I pulled at the denim stretched tight around my thighs. "I don't even fit in *my* jeans." I, too, love puns. For me, they hide real feelings. A bad pun is a good cover-up.

"Dear—your genes are fine. You look just like me."

And in an odd way I *did*: thick blonde straight hair, hers in a braided chignon and mine in a braid or a ponytail to my waist, blue eyes, pale, almost white eyebrows, and delicate fair skin.

Anyway, my genes surely were shrunk or microwaved or morphed. Because my mother stands six feet tall!

Next to her I looked like a swollen miniature. The eighth dwarf: Plumpy.

This conversation with my mother struggled to its usual discouraging dead end, and I went up to my room. I had to finish my report on Harriet Beecher Stowe.

But first I locked my door and wrote my letter to Ann Landers. . . .

On Monday morning my mother tiptoed in at seven, her regular time to get me up for school. "Morning, Asa love," she whispered. Though she was pregnant (we were all incredibly happy about that), she was so slim you could hardly tell.

Looking at my tall, graceful mother, I was glad I had written the letter to Ann Landers. I had it hidden, all sealed and stamped, in my looseleaf. Still, because I felt guilty about writing it, I wanted to make sure she wouldn't find it. She was supersensitive.

Like what happened last Christmas. When I asked for my own radio alarm, she was really hurt. "But *I'm* your waker-upper. I'm more reliable than any electrical appliance," she argued. She *liked* taking care of me, and she wasn't giving it up.

Now, she kissed me on the top of my head. "Time to get up."

Once she was sure I was up, she left, and I washed my face and brushed my teeth while she made breakfast for my father. He always leaves for work very early because he likes to start the school day with the *IN* basket on his desk empty.

Fifteen minutes later she was back with THE TRAY.

The tray is a wooden rectangle about twelve by eighteen inches with really neat movable sides that turn up into small walls while it's being carried, but snap down into a stand when someone is eating. It was designed and built by my father when I was a skinny, sickly kid, so that I could eat in bed.

Somehow, my mother neglected to notice that those days were gone forever, and my father was too busy being a principal for it to matter.

Mom loved serving me breakfast in bed. Each day the tray was covered with an embroidered doily and had a small surprise on it, a fresh flower from our garden or a cartoon or a funny news clipping about a blind dog who found his way hundreds of miles to his home or a genius baby who did algebra at birth. Or a flake who saw Elvis at some mall.

Her favorite news stories had to do with UFOs or people who remembered living centuries ago when they were kings and queens or vampires. My mother bought *The Star* and *The Enquirer* in the supermarket just for these weird tales.

More important, the tray always had an incredible breakfast on it—fresh-squeezed orange juice and then some gigantic main dish—walnut or berry pancakes, or sausages and eggs, or hot muffins and cream cheese, and always milk and tarts or brownies or doughnuts.

Only my best friend, Felicia, knew my breakfast secret. When I'd told her, she was totally amazed. "You could be in *The Guinness Book of World Records*," she said, and she closed her eyes and composed the entry. "*Asa Andersen, age twelve, eats breakfast in bed every single day. She has never tasted CHEERIOS, CAP'N KRUNCH or any other cold cereal. She has never had frozen pancakes, or waffles, or POP TARTS. Not once.*

"I could get you in. I'll ask my father to send it to Guinness," she offered. "You'll be famous."

"Yeah, great idea. Then the whole world will know I'm a freak."

"Not a freak." She was quiet for a minute. "But you're right. Only Prince William and movie stars and people like that are supposed to live that way. How did this happen to you?"

"I was born nine weeks too early and very tiny. The doctors weren't sure I'd live. Then I had asthma for years and years, and every so often I'd just stop breathing. That caused lots of excitement."

"But now—" Felicia argued, "—you're healthy as a horse. A healthy horse."

"I outgrew it—with the help of miracle drugs."

"—And the sick treatment is still going on? Principals—and their wives—are supposed to be smart people."

"You can say that again."

She did, but so sarcastically she made me laugh.

This morning there were two sizzling sausages alongside eggs sunny-side up.

Mom drew the blinds and let in the morning light.

"How'd you sleep?" she asked.

"With my eyes closed." It was my favorite answer. Sometimes I substituted, "Under the covers," or "Over the covers," or "Horizontal."

You'd think after so many years she would have stopped asking.

"How are you this morning, my dear?" she followed up.

"Sleepy," I said. Sometimes I chose one of the other dwarfs: "Bashful, Dopey, Grumpy, Happy." I saved Sneezy for when I had a cold, and I *never* used Doc because that would have sent my mother searching for symptoms.

She went off, and when she returned for the tray she did the usual. "You're not going to leave that lonely sausage," she teased. "Come on, Asa, clean plate club. Do it for Mom."

And, even with the letter to Ann Landers all written, guess what? I did it for Mom.

THE TERRIBLE PART WAS THAT I LOVED TO EAT.

I COULD EAT ANYTHING ANYTIME.

I WAS AN EATING MACHINE OUT OF CONTROL.

I DIDN'T WANT TO BE, BUT IT WAS SO TEMPTING, AND IT WAS WHAT MOM WANTED.

My dad ate a lot, too, but he jogged and worked it off. My mother had a good appetite but she said it was her metabolism that kept her slim—except now, of course, because she was pregnant.

Maybe it was all her worrying about me eating that really burned up her calories.

I had to face it: I was a walking garbage disposal unit, gulping everything down. Sometimes I could actually hear my stomach grinding away. And when I ate too much, I didn't feel like doing much, so I took it easy.

When I couldn't stuff another bite in my face, my mother took the tray away and I got ready to go to school.

On Queens Boulevard, I stood by the mailbox and stared at it. But I couldn't make myself drop the letter in. It ended up torn into shreds—I didn't even save the stamp. By the time I reached Felicia's house, I was keeping tears back by blinking fast.

Her grandma stood in the doorway. I waved hello. Felicia was waiting on the front steps, her black curly hair and dark eyes shining in the sun. She was the prettiest girl in the class and my best friend.

Most kids at school were leery of me—the principal's daughter. They kept their distance. But not Felicia. Once I'd asked her, "How come you're not afraid to be my friend?"

"I like to mix with the big shots," was her answer, and we both cracked up.

Now, all she needed was one look at my droopy face. "Hi. I bet you just *didn't* mail another letter to Ann Landers?"

I nodded.

"Boy, you waste a lot of paper. I told you the only way is to talk to your mother."

"I tried. You know what? She thinks I'm beautiful."

"You are very pretty. Skinny isn't everything."

"Not you, too," I groaned. "Pul-*leeze*."

"Did you try your father?"

"He'd only tell me I'm descended from the Valkyries."

"The what?" Felicia wrinkled her nose.

"Ancient beautiful maidens who served the gods. Then he'd send me back to Mom. He's too busy. Besides, they agreed when she quit working that my health was mainly her department."

Felicia shook her head. My family puzzled her. Her own mother was dead, so her grandmother and father were raising her. But Felicia's grandmother was boss.

I put out my hand pretending to read my palm. "I see the future fifty years from now. An old blonde fat lady is waddling around on a cane. People stare at her and whisper, 'That's Asa Andersen. Boy, is she huge. How did she ever get to be *that* big? She must have been born that way.

"'Nah. You'll never believe this, but she was a premature baby. A shrimp. Very, very undersized.

"'That blimp was tiny? You can't be serious.' They'll cluck their tongues in wonder. 'How could such a thing happen? Her folks must have overfed her for years. Why didn't someone do something about it?'"

It was agony to imagine all this.

"I don't see what else you can do," Felicia said. "You should have mailed your letter to Ann Landers."

We turned the corner onto the school block.

Another sixth-grader—Sandra White—was walking ahead of us. I would have died rather than have her hear our conversation. I signaled silence with my finger across my lips.

Our pace was quick, so in a minute we were passing her. *"Buenos días,"* Felicia said as we moved by. *"¿Como está usted?"* She was a New Yorker and her English was perfectly good, but Sandra had snubbed her earlier in the month, leaving her out of a party. (She'd even invited me, but I didn't go.) Sandra couldn't bear that Felicia was so pretty, but Felicia believed the slight was because she was Puerto Rican. So she spoke Spanish to Sandra whenever she could, mystifying her. Rubbing it in her face.

When we were well ahead of Sandra, Felicia repeated, "You should have mailed the letter. I don't see what else you can do."

"I'll have to think of something," I said desperately. "Nobody, not even Ann Landers can help me. *I* have to help myself!"

"Way to go!" Felicia said. "You're smart enough!"

She believed in me. That's the way good friends are.

2

Enter the Tarheel

"**M**y report is ready," I told Felicia, as we hung up our jackets, "and, boy, am I glad I'm not first."

School activities mostly went alphabetically by last name. "Andersen" had been the only "A" until sixth grade. Until Anita Acharya came from New Delhi, India.

Each of us had researched a person who greatly influenced history. We were going to give oral reports first, and then hand in the written work.

Felicia was curious. "How many pages is yours?"

"Eight."

"Eight? Miss Kahn said five and up."

"Harriet Beecher Stowe is really interesting."

"So is Sojourner Truth. But she is interesting exactly five pages worth. Exactly."

"*You* are not the principal's daughter."

"He *made* you do a long report?"

"No. I guess it's in my blood."

"Between the genes and the blood, my friend, what part of you is the *you* you?"

I gave her a sick smile, and we took our seats, I in the middle of the first row, and Felicia in the second row further back. Miss Kahn began the roll call that started each school day.

One absentee. Tommy Lee. He would come; he was always late.

Then it was report time. Anita headed for the front of the room, trading places with Miss Kahn. Just as Anita was settling in the teacher's chair, the door opened and in the doorway stood a strange boy carrying a bunch of registration papers in his hand, and alongside him stood—guess who? Tommy Lee.

Like everyone else in the room, I took a good look at the newcomer—and my heart turned into a tom-tom. *Bang!* it went. *Bang, bang, bang!*

Tommy, confused at seeing Anita up front, looked around for the teacher. Anita quickly returned to her own seat as Miss Kahn, her face stern, headed to the front of the room again.

Tommy whispered something in her ear.

"Your attention, everyone," Miss Kahn called. She

was one of those teachers who believed in openness in the classroom. No secret discussions; no locking kids out.

"This is Robert Edward Lee, Tommy's cousin, who's just moved up here from the South. He hopes to join our class."

"He's a Tarheel, too," Tommy added, grinning. Tommy, who had bright red hair, was class clown. He'd say or do anything for a laugh. He owned an ugly black rubber snake and a brown plastic rat that he loved to sneak into girls' lunch boxes or gym bags. His hair made him the way he was—it's hard to be serious if your head glows.

Tommy looked at us wickedly. "Now y'all get a pair of Tarheels for the price of one."

A few of his buddies thought that was funny. Tommy loved talking about being a Tarheel, but he couldn't say why North Carolinians were called that.

"Tommy," Miss Kahn said, "it's twenty past nine. I'm developing a theory that your heels *stick* to the ground every step you take, and *that's* what makes you a Tarheel."

"I have an excuse, Ma'am. I was helping him register—"

"You always have an excuse, Tommy. You and he could have gone in earlier. Anyway, thank you for your efforts. You can sit down now, while I talk to your cousin about our class."

She moved a chair next to the desk so *he* could sit, then she sat down and talked to him.

I stared, trying to look like I wasn't staring, and I found myself breathing faster. Like the old asthma days.

He was definitely out of this world. An extra-terrestrial. He had brown hair that stood up in a cow-lick and a sprinkling of freckles across his nose and cheeks as though he'd been lightly dusted with cinnamon. His large dark eyes were framed by thick brown lashes.

I was so glad I was wearing a long sweater and my black jeans. It was my most thinning outfit.

"All right, class." Miss Kahn clapped her hands to get our attention. "We've got all the registering business done, and now I want you to welcome Robert Edward Lee."

Mmmm, I thought enthusiastically. *Mr. Perfect.* I joined the chorus. "Welcome to Class 6-404. We're glad to have you here, Robert Edward Lee." (This baby system was Miss Kahn's idea for our learning newcomers' names.)

On my right, I heard Ramon Ortiz, who often stuttered. His words now were loud and clear. It was odd how Ramon could speak in a group or sing beautifully in the school chorus. Only when he spoke alone did he have trouble.

Felicia had a major crush on Ramon. She loved his curly brown hair and his velvety dark skin. But he didn't talk to girls. For months, she had been trying to figure out a way to get him to talk to her—in Spanish.

"I bet in Spanish he doesn't stutter," she said. "I could help him so he was comfortable in English. He could practice with me. Then he wouldn't stutter."

"Why don't you just speak to him in Spanish?" I suggested. "Tell him what you think."

"Because he is *Cubano.* Cuban. And sometimes Cubanos think they are better than Puerto Ricans."

"You're crazy. Ramon would never snub you. I see him looking at you sometimes. He likes you."

"I wouldn't take the chance," Felicia said. "He has to come to me."

Standing beside the teacher, the new boy was almost as tall as she was. He was thin but with muscles. He looked like an athlete.

Remarkable. Sixth grade boys, as Felicia liked to say, were "nothing to write home about." (Felicia had eleven cousins in San Juan she was always writing to.)

The boys in 6-404 were nice enough classmates, but they were short and shapeless, and they broadened instead of narrowing at the middle. They hadn't hit their growth spurts yet.

Who was I to talk? I understood better than anyone. I was going to grow up to wear Queen Size dresses. Even though my mother said I was stunning.

"Robert, take the vacant seat right behind Asa," Miss Kahn's hand indicated the direction.

A shudder of pleasure charged through me, and I sat up higher and straighter in my seat. My hands actually trembled and there was a whooshing in my head. I kept my eyes on my desk. Love at first sight: Romeo and Juliet; that Italian poet Dante, my father once told me about, who first saw his beloved Beatrice when he was *nine* and she was *eight!* One look was all those guys needed. One look was enough for me, too.

I had wondered a lot about love. How did it feel? Closest I ever came was the supermarket check-out boy with sideburns. I admired him so much, I'd buy each item separately so I could keep getting back on his line. But I'd never been hit like this.

"Behind *who?*"

I looked up. The perfect boy's face had a frown on it.

"Asa Andersen. Please, Asa, raise your hand."

I did.

He objected. "Asa's not a girl's name. I've got an uncle—Asa Davis Lee—back home in Winston-Salem."

Some of my classmates thought that piece of information was hilarious. To me it was tragic.

"In this class, Asa is a girl's name," Miss Kahn said. "Robert, please take your seat."

He began heading very slowly in my direction. Like he was moving toward the Electric Chair. Very, *very* slowly. Maybe Miss Kahn was right about the sticky heels of Tarheels?

I hated his uncle.

"All right, Anita. Come forward and please try again."

"Yes. I have chosen to speak about a great Hindu, a great Indian leader. But before I start I have a favor to ask. My father is opening a new restaurant in Times Square, and we would like a good American name for it. If you think of one, please tell me afterward. It would help us so much."

She opened her folder. "Today I shall speak about the person I have the most admiration for—Mahatma Gandhi."

"I love that name—Mahatma," I called out impulsively. "It sounds like a dance—the Mahatma?" I covered my mouth too late. I blame my father for this first stupid misstep. He taught me to appreciate words and their sounds.

"It means Great Soul, Asa," Anita said reproachfully.

"It is not a *dance*. Mahatma was the nickname given him by the Indian people."

Anita was so stiff, she must never have misbehaved in her life. She and Mei, who came from China, were the best mannered students in the class. But Mei sometimes would giggle. Not Anita. She never seemed to relax.

She had the most glorious accent. Like she was a British movie star. I wanted to be friends.

"Sorry," I said. I hadn't meant to offend. "It's really a nice nickname."

Anita went on to tell about Gandhi, whom she was now calling Gandhiji. Indian names are slippery. They change.

"This remarkable man set out to free India from its British rulers without violence. He did not believe in bloodshed. So he taught the people *satyagraha*." She printed it on the board. "It means passive resistance or civil disobedience: If you think a law is unjust, don't obey it."

"Wow," Felicia said. "Can you give us an example?"

"Yes. When the British put a heavy tax on salt that was a burden to poor Indians, they did not pay the tax. Gandhiji led a march to the sea and they extracted salt from the water."

"I didn't know you could do that," Tommy said.

"He also helped lead India to freedom by fasting."

She lost Tommy there. "Oh, come on. How can you fight soldiers by fasting? You just get weaker."

"Well, he did! He went on a hunger strike for weeks. The British were afraid he would die, and then his people would be so angry at his death there would be a revolt.

"Millions of Indians would rise up furiously against their colonial rulers. Whether or not you believe it, Gandhi's fasting finally made the British army pack up and go home."

My ears were instantly alert during this exchange.

Anita concluded with great pride, "Gandhiji made them quit India! And the great Dr. Martin Luther King learned to use Gandhi's *satyagraha*, too, in the struggle for civil rights."

She passed a picture of her hero around.

When it was my turn, I studied the picture of the great man. He was wearing only a white cloth wrapped around the lower half of his body. Anita called it a *dhoti*.

I saw a bent old man leaning on a stick. He was so skinny his bones stuck out. *He* went weeks without eating! He didn't look in the least remarkable, yet he was truly amazing.

And, it occurred to me, if he could defeat an entire

army by fasting, maybe I could defeat my mother the same way.

I felt a rush of affection for him. Like an electric shock.

Mahatma, I stared into those wise old eyes, and I made a weird silent pledge: *The way you liberated millions in India, I will liberate myself. I will learn from you. I have no choice.*

I would have liked to keep the picture, but, of course, I had to pass it on. I handed it to Ramon.

My excitement remained. Like an explorer or a scientist on the edge of a discovery, I suddenly felt confident because I had decided what my next step had to be.

I knew *exactly* what I had to do.

I was so out of it, I hardly heard Miss Kahn's comment, "There was a lot more to the British withdrawal from India than Gandhi's fasting, of course, and we'll talk about that later. Thank you, Anita. Well done." Then my classmates were applauding, and it was my turn.

I picked up my materials and hurried forward.

"I chose Harriet Beecher Stowe," I started, "because I admire *Uncle Tom's Cabin* and also because through it she changed America's history."

Then I went on to sketch out her childhood quickly,

leaving out all the boring dates and stuff. "She was the brilliant daughter of a famous preacher, who said about her when she was eight, 'Hattie is a genius. I would give a hundred dollars if she was a boy.'"

Some of the boys stamped their feet and hooted. Tommy giggled till he ended up coughing. The girls remained silent. I waited for quiet, then I told how her mother died when she was very young, how she loved to read and write, and how she grew up to teach school.

"She never lived in the South though she did once visit a plantation where there were slaves.

"But her father and brothers were anti-slavery and she married a Bible teacher, who was also an abolitionist. Slavery was on her mind even though she was a busy mother of five, and a journalist and writer whose family depended on her earnings."

I paused. "This is the best part. For years she was against slavery, but she didn't act. Then one Sunday in 1851, while she was in church, a scene flashed into her mind. Like a play on stage."

"Or a video," Sandra called out.

I nodded. "It was the image of a white man forcing two slaves to flog an old black man to death. She could almost hear the old man praying as he died.

"She went home and wrote that scene down. Her husband was away so she read what she'd written to her two sons, twelve and ten years old. After she read, they broke down sobbing and one of them said, 'Oh mama! Slavery is the most cruel thing in the world.' That was the beginning of her writing the book."

Robert Edward Lee had his hand raised. *I was going to be the first girl in the class he talked to!*

"I don't think she changed history one bit," he challenged me. "Everyone knew the war was coming."

I stood my ground. "President Lincoln said it. When he met Mrs. Stowe in 1862, his exact words were, 'So you're the little woman who started this great war.' If President Lincoln said so, that's good enough for me."

The Tarheel was shaking his head *no.* I took no notice. Him against Lincoln? No contest.

I picked up my copy of *Uncle Tom's Cabin*, which had pictures of Uncle Tom and kind Mr. Shelby and Simon Legree and Liza and Topsy and Eva, and passed it around. Then I returned to my seat, amidst applause.

I'd enjoyed writing the report and even liked giving it aloud. Bad luck the new boy didn't feel the same way.

"Well done," Miss Kahn said. "I look forward to reading these reports." She meant it.

I truly loved being in my last year in my father's school. Not that he ran a bad school. On the contrary. Miss Kahn was a terrific teacher; in fact, most of the teachers were good. My father saw to that. Still, being the principal's daughter was a drag.

The kids were a real United Nations. Their parents had come from all over the world to find better lives.

In Queens, New York, the immigrant borough.

That lunchtime Felicia began to tease me. "Lucky you! You get to sit with that new boy behind you."

I didn't say a word about the tom-tom heartbeats, or Juliet, or Beatrice. A few things you can't tell even your best friend. "Oh, I might introduce you to him after a while," I said airily. "Once I get to know him better."

"That's why I'm your friend, big shot," Felicia winked. "You know all the important people."

"That's why you're my friend *now*," I said. "But soon you'll have other reasons. Better reasons. You are going to want to hang out with me because I'm so thin and beautiful."

"Really? You figured out a way?"

I nodded.

"*Buena suerte*," she said gravely. "Good luck."

I daydreamed for hours that afternoon. At dismissal time, Miss Kahn kept me to talk about Harriet Beecher Stowe, whose writing she admired.

When I got downstairs into the school lobby just inside the front doors, there *he* was, kneeling and tying his shoelace while his cousin waited. They both had their backs to me.

I was sure they'd hear my heart thumping it was so loud in my own ears. But not loud enough to drown out their words.

As I passed behind them, I caught the end of a question.

"—kind of crazy Yankee idea to name a girl Asa? *Asa?*" And the two of them began to snigger.

I got out of there before they could see me.

3

What's
In a Name?

"**H**ah! Does he think *his* name is poetry or something?" Felicia, waiting outside, was indignant. "It's a nothing name. What's so special about *Robert Edward Lee?* It's dry. Prickly. Like a cactus plant. No flowers."

I was really down.

"Wait till he hears *my* whole name, Asa."

She had a name to love: Felicia Esperanza Aurora Rodriguez. Felicia meant happiness, Esperanza meant hope, Aurora meant dawn. She was very proud of all her names.

"He better believe my initials!" she continued. "F-E-A-R."

"Tell me the truth, Felicia. Do you think I have a crazy name?"

"No. I think your name sounds nice! *Asa Andersen.*"

She pronounced it softly. "All those 'A' sounds in a row are neat."

"That's alliteration," I said dispiritedly. "Big deal."

"What?"

"My father explained it to me. When the first sounds in words near each other get repeated, that's alliteration."

"Your father has a word for everything. What does Asa mean?"

"I don't think it means anything. I never asked. There's something worse. I have a middle name."

"Oh?"

"I don't use it unless I have to."

"What is it?"

"Get ready. *Alfifa!*" I whispered it. "That's the first time I've ever told anybody. Imagine? *Alfifa!*"

Felicia was a real loyal friend. She didn't laugh. "Your family really goes in for that alliteration stuff."

"I might as well tell you the rest," I said miserably.

"Oh, come on," she groaned. "You've got more names?"

"No. No more names, but when I was learning to write my father showed me another way—the original way—of spelling Alfifa." I rooted around in my pocket for a pencil and a scrap of paper and I wrote: ÆLGIFU. "That's the way it was written in Olde English long ago, the A and E joined together."

Felicia squinted at it. "It looks like a sneeze. I want to say, *Salud! Dios te bendiga.*" She shook her head. ÆLGIFU was too much for her.

" 'Two letters like that are called a ligature,' my father says. I think they should be called a *leg*ature. It looks like the two letters have broken legs and are tied in a splint."

Felicia laughed. I carefully tore the scrap of paper into the tiniest confetti so no one, *no one*, could piece it together. "*My* initials are A-A-A," I said disgustedly. "Automobile Association of America. Makes you think of—"

"Tow trucks," Felicia said, at the exact same second I did, and we locked pinkies. We were such good friends we often thought of the same things at the same time. Sometimes we didn't even have to say them aloud. We thought them together.

I dropped Felicia off at her house and went on my way. I tried to think about other things, but couldn't. *What kind of crazy Yankee idea to name a girl Asa?*

Mr. Perfect was not so perfect.

Maybe I hadn't heard right? No. I'd heard.

I felt such a fool because all that afternoon, when he'd sat behind me never making a sound, I'd tried to concentrate on my schoolwork, but I couldn't. I concentrated on him.

He's new, I'd thought, and he doesn't know New

York manners. He's probably shy. I'll help him. I'll make the first move. But it has to be the right first move.

Then I'd begun to consider possibilities. I could discover a dollar bill under my seat and ask him it he'd lost it. But if he said yes, I'd have to give it to him. His cousin Tommy would say yes in such a case. It was too risky.

I could faint. That's the oldest trick in the book. But I really didn't know how. Collapse at the knees or fall on my face? Make a fool of myself.

I could drop my book and wait for him to pick it up, and then I'd thank him and we'd be talking. Too obvious. Why wouldn't I pick up my own book?

If he sneezed, I could say "God bless you!" He hadn't sneezed or sniffled once; what were the odds?

Then I'd had another idea. I'd tell him about the public library and ask him if he wanted to join . . .

The dismissal bell had interrupted this long reverie before I could actually *do* anything. Bless the dismissal bell. Because then I came downstairs and heard the *real* him saying his hateful words about my name.

I mooched along toward home slower than a camel carrying heavy nomads and their bundles. I avoided every crack, mindful of the old jingle "Step on a crack/Break your mother's back." Not that I believed it. But I wanted my mom to be okay.

It was a cloudy afternoon. The sun dimmed and the sky began to look as though it might rain. A cold gray drizzle began. That was the way I felt at the moment: gloomy, drippy, blah.

I wished I had an ordinary name.

Maybe the rain would turn into a storm so fierce it would carry me away above the clouds to a place where kids—particularly boys—were always kind. Fantasyland.

At that moment I would have traded for almost any other name, that is for any *regular* name: Jane or Beth would have made me skip for joy. Linda would have sent me turning cartwheels. Mary won the Oscar for best of all because it was wonderfully plain.

"Mary," I said, trying it out softly, tasting the wholesomeness of it.

But I was forever Asa, which rhymes with nothing in English, but with *mesa* and *cabeza* in Spanish.

My name had never troubled me before. Oh, once in a while I wondered why I never met another girl with the same name. But I had too many other things to think about. Like:

Would my skin stay smooth or would I end up with zits? (I had a tube of Clearasil buried in my dresser drawer, in case. . . .)

Would my mother have a girl or a boy?

How would it feel to have so much money you didn't know how much you had?

How long would it take to lose twenty pounds?

Would adding and subtracting fractions ever get easier?

Would someone ever want to marry me? How would he be smart enough to know I was the one?

Thoughts like these flickered in and out of my mind like fireflies, but I didn't really worry about them.

Most frequent flicker was the sibling question: Baby sister or baby brother? Secretly, I preferred a sister; I'd take whatever I got, of course.

But all of this was wondering, not worrying.

Now the Tarheel and his mean words really got to me. As I scuffed along, one of my mother's favorite sayings clicked into my mind like a slide on a screen.

Appearances are deceptive.

All grown-ups repeated these kinds of things over and over: *Beauty is skin deep. Handsome is as handsome does.*

Words offered as warning signals, constant parental beepers in the background. I'd paid very little attention to them.

But my mother was sure right about this one.

What had looked like a skyrocket had turned out to be a dud. Instead of lighting up the place it had fizzled and brought gloom.

I guess I should listen to Mom a little more, I thought. Thinking that was easier than doing it.

Walking around the house to the back door, I sniffed and knew instantly that my mother had been baking *krumkaker*. The air was sweet with the scent of curled cookies.

She shaped the dough around teacups and then baked the crusts till they were flaky. When they cooled, they were delicious shells waiting to be filled with ice cream or whipped cream. Now—if the Tarheel had only been nicer . . .

"Hi, Mom—" I thumped in. Surrounded by the baking smells, I saw the *krumkaker* spread out to cool on the kitchen table, but there was no sign of my mother. A note lay amidst the cups and cookies:

Dear Asa,

I'm upstairs resting. A sample of the baking is waiting for you in the refrigerator. I need the opinion of my royal taster.

Love,
Mom

A real royal taster had to test all the food prepared for a king to see if it was poisoned. If the taster got sick or died—too bad—the king merely ate something else.

Royal Taster Asa ran no risk; she simply got to sample all the best dishes first. And then finish them. No risk—except getting fatter and fatter.

I lifted the whipped cream-filled pastry out of the refrigerator and set it on the counter. A peak of fresh cream was topped with chocolate sprinkles and a cherry.

It was scary coming home afternoons to notes in an empty kitchen. My mother was having a difficult pregnancy. She didn't throw up anymore, but she spent a lot of time lying down, and our neighbor, Mrs. Larson, came in to do the laundry and heavy cleaning. Mom's eyes were shadowed and she was easily tired.

This was scary because Nora Andersen—Mom— had been the most enthusiastic and energetic wife and mother in Woodside, Queens. Do-it-yourself Nora!

She had taught third-grade till I came along, and she could do—and did—incredibly wonderful domestic things all through my childhood.

She changed washers and fixed leaky pipes; she did carpentry; she grew herbs: basil and parsley and thyme; and she raised gorgeous dahlias and roses. She enjoyed doing all that stuff.

"You're looking at a member of the most endangered American species: a Housewife!" she reminded us regularly.

It was a joke, but a serious joke.

"We Homemakers will be microwaved off the earth. Zapped! We're passé—like the dodo bird."

The dodo bird?

I went and looked up the dodo bird in the encyclopedia. It was a clumsy, stupid bird about the size of a swan. Nobody liked it. It wasn't pretty and it couldn't fly. It ate seeds and leaves and swallowed large rocks to help its digestion.

Large rocks! It's extinct now. No wonder.

"You're no dodo bird," I told my mother. "No way."

"I'm glad you feel like that, Asa, but yours is a minority opinion."

On Mother's Day, a couple of years ago, we bought her a food processor—because she loves to cook and that would save her work. It diced the onions so she wouldn't have to chop and cry, and it pureed the leeks and did a lot of other dirty work. When she saw it, she said, "The government ought to put us *Homemakers* on a reservation. We're obsolete. There's no need for us anymore."

I couldn't believe it when she stored away that food processor. Never *once* did she use it. Instead, she went right on dicing onions and garlic by hand, tears streaming down.

To all our teasing her about being old-fashioned, she answered, "Cooking is not so simple. People in other countries understand that. Did you know that in Japan the best noodles are cut by hand so that they're perfectly made? There are people who are noodle masters. When ordinary people meet a master, they bow low with respect and say, 'Greetings, Noodle-Master.'"

This struck me as hilarious. I began to bow real low to my mother. "Greetings, Noodle-Master. I've come to slurp oodles of noodles. My goal is to be a noodle-head."

She laughed, but she didn't change her mind. "Cooking is an art," she said, "and you can't produce art by machine."

She's a sincere, terrific, loving mother. So why *couldn't* she see me in the present? Instead of seeing me the way I used to be? A shrimp. Delicate. Asthmatic.

I stuck my pinkie into the whipped cream. I almost licked it and then I stopped myself. Pig! I quickly washed my hands and then set the cake back in the refrigerator.

I was perfectly healthy. I took phys. ed. like other kids. Earlier this year, I'd worked for hours and hours learning to swing across the gym from ring-to-ring. It hadn't been easy but now I was better than many of the girls in my class. Felicia, watching me, said, "Your name should be Tarzana not Asa." Felicia was scared to use the rings at first—she's very brave except about heights; she hates all high places—but she practiced with me and she managed okay. She'll never be crazy about it, though.

I love aerial exercises for the wonderful light feeling that comes with flying through the air. That must be why birds sing.

At home, I dared not tell about swinging on the rings. My mother would be terrified and she'd make my father arrange for a modified P.E. program.

I DIDN'T WANT A MODIFIED ANY-THING PROGRAM!
I WANTED TO BE NORMAL!

I could glide up and down those ropes like an orangutan. I thought I just might be a firefighter when I grew up.

Climbing up and sliding down were fun. I could do backflips, as many as six in a row. I'd worked up to six by practicing on the soft Rya rug in my room. My goal was ten.

I wasn't graceful, but I bent and stretched and squatted and grunted to music as well as anyone. I still exercised every night. If only I didn't eat so much . . .

Since I hadn't been allowed heavy activity in the early grades, I was glad to be part of it. I liked being ordinary and not noticeable.

All during those first school years, I'd sat on the side and watched the games and dreamed about playing: jumping rope cleanly to break the record in Double Dutch; knocking the volleyball back hard; or cracking my bat against the ball and rounding the bases to score a home run in softball.

Best of all, shooting baskets on the outdoor court in the sunlight with a tall cute boy telling me how good I was. A boy who might easily have resembled this new boy!

My father was a runner.

My mother had been an avid tennis player till I was born.

Then—worrying about me became her single sport; she qualified as a World-Class Worrier. If anyone ever started a Watch-and-Worry Hall of Fame for mothers in Cooperstown, New York, Nora Andersen would be the first one elected.

And THE TRAY could be her trophy.

I had been a spectator on the sidelines all through the early years of school. There were plenty of other fat, sick, or lazy kids, so I wasn't noticeable.

But by the middle of fifth grade I was healthy, and I

wanted out. Or in. Whatever. And I began to feel freaky. Worse: I knew I had M.T.

Mother Trouble.

I wasn't an extreme M.T. case. Every day on TV and in the newspapers, there were awful stories about parents who really abused kids. Or crazy sick parents who even killed kids. So what did I have to complain about? *Breakfast in bed?*

That's what made my situation hopeless. My mother was one of the best mothers in the world. She was kind and thoughtful; she devoted her life to taking care of me and my father, mainly *me* because of my crummy beginning.

I longed to shout at her, "Supermom! Enough. Lay off. I need a little space."

But the words stayed bottled up inside me.

She was my mother, after all.

4

Gandhi Is Dandy

"**D**ad?" My burning question wouldn't wait, so, even though he was doing his last-minute packing, I went up and knocked on his door. "I need to ask you something."

"Come in. I'm just finishing up here."

I went in. "Why did you and Mom name me Asa?"

That surprised him. "Why do you ask?"

"I was just wondering."

"It's a traditional Scandinavian name."

"How could that be? I never met another Asa."

"That's because people don't know their own history. If they did, you'd be meeting Asas left and right."

That was a hoot. "I doubt it, Daddy. Left and right?"

"Is there some special reason why you're asking tonight?"

I wouldn't squeal on the Tarheel. Besides, my father didn't encourage tales out of school. I shook my head.

"I'm pleased you've begun to think about your name. Mom and I knew you would, and we've waited patiently."

"It's a strange name, Dad."

"No," he disagreed. "It's a very famous name."

"If famous was what you were going for, why didn't you name me Pippi Longstocking Andersen? That's probably the most famous Scandinavian girl's name."

"You're wrong. Pippi is an upstart. Asa goes way back. I'm talking a thousand years."

Uh uh. His eyes got that funny glow that appears whenever he talks about *our people's history*. (His family came from Denmark and Mom's from Norway.)

He spends every free minute reading about the Norse. (Norse means old Scandinavian.) He's writing a family history, and he talks so much about it, my mother likes to tease and say he's a "Norse wind."

But she's interested in all that stuff, too. In a way, she's worse. She's collecting *herring* recipes that go back centuries for a cookbook. I think she should call it *The Stinky Cookbook*. She likes the title *Something Fishy*. Boy, do I hate herring!

"Was Asa a real woman?"

"Of course. She was a queen. Be proud of your

name," he said. "It's a noble, ancient name. A historic name. Any Scandinavian woman should be honored by it. And that goes for Alfifa as well."

I gulped. Then I hurried to call Felicia.

"Felicia? My father just told me where they got my name."

"Where?"

"From history. Asa was a great queen more than a thousand years ago."

That brought dead silence at the other end.

"Felicia?"

"I'm impressed, Your Highness."

"Come on, you like the name Madonna a lot, and that's older."

"Actually it's sort of sweet," Felicia said, "that your folks went to so much trouble to find you a name."

"Yeah, but a lot of good it will do me with that bat-brain who sits behind me."

"Look, just make up your mind you won't let him push you around." That's as far as Felicia got.

"Dinner—" my mother's voice interrupted us "— just enough time to get to the airport."

Mom had cooked my father's favorite meal: A smorgasbord—a hot and cold buffet of fish, meats, cheeses, salads, casserole—all the foods he loved. The smells were heavenly, but I mostly tried to eat salad. It was hard. Frankly, I don't know what rabbits see in lettuce. I'd rather be a squirrel and eat nuts any day.

Then we drove to Kennedy Airport. And the second the wheels of my dad's plane left the ground—I gave up eating.

Only my mother didn't know it till the next morning. Though my first words were, "I'm not hungry," she insisted on bringing up the tray: French toast and fresh strawberries.

"I can't, Mom," I said. "I just can't eat breakfast. I feel full. I'll barf if you make me eat."

She took my temperature, and, though it was normal, she decided to drive me to school. We stopped for Felicia, who was surprised when my agitated mother said, "Asa didn't eat a crumb for breakfast, Felicia. She's coming down with something. Please look after her in school."

"Sure," Felicia said. "No problem."

"I'll pick you up at three, Asa. Don't do anything strenuous today," my mother warned. "No gym."

Please God, don't let her walk into the office and make a fuss, I prayed. And God heard.

Once she drove away, I explained, "I am not going to eat anything until she understands."

Felicia was impressed. "You think you can hold out all day?"

"As many days as I have to."

"Asa, that's crazy."

"Did you see that old man, Gandhi? If he could do it, I can do it. The British thought he was crazy, too."

I was hungry but happy. Lunch hour was hard, so to avoid all the good food smells we went out into the schoolyard. Mei joined us.

We were sitting on a bench talking when Felicia discovered a big wad of gum stuck to the end of my braid, dangling like a fat squishy pink pompom. "Two packs of DUBBLE BUBBLE at least," she estimated. "Lucky your hair wasn't hanging free in a ponytail. You hold the braid steady," she told Mei, and she slowly managed to pull the hair free of the wad of gum. "There. I got most of it off," she said finally, "but the ends are still gummy."

"We can use my manicuring scissors for trimming," Mei suggested. They worked together on it, this time Felicia holding and Mei snipping. When I saw the handful of pink-tipped blonde hair, I felt really angry. It was a third-grade trick, an idiot kid trick. And I'd lost about an inch of hair.

I was sad. I had *never* had my hair cut in my whole life!

"Who would do such a dumb thing?" Mei wondered.

"Some moron. I don't know who," I said, which was a fib. I knew who.

On our way back inside, I whispered to Felicia, "That rotten Tarheel."

"You don't *know* he did it," Felicia argued. "Anyway, if he wanted to be mean he could have stuck the gum higher up and ruined all your hair."

"*He* did it," I said, "and I'll pay him back."

That afternoon during the English Drill, when it was his turn at the board, he got the sentence: *Coming down to brakefast, my mother made us go back and comb our hairs.* First, he just stood there as if the words were in a foreign language. Then he fixed *breakfast* and *hair.* "Good so far," Miss Kahn said.

"There's more?" He was bewildered.

Oh yes. I raised my hand and waved it madly, and Miss Kahn called on me.

"It's simple," I said, moving up to take the chalk right out of his hand. He didn't part with it easily. "The sentence starts with a dangling participle, which makes it sound like the mother was coming down to breakfast. It should start *When we were coming down. . . .* We is the subject."

I rewrote it correctly.

"Thank you," Miss Kahn said to both of us. We started toward our seats.

"Show-off," he muttered.

"Well, I guess if your brain is gummy . . ." I retorted, and then watched him scramble to get away from me.

I brought my lunch bag home untouched. I could have given the food away or tossed it, but I wanted to make a point to my mother—*No More Overfeeding!*

She took one look at the lunch bag and ordered me to lie down and rest all afternoon.

At dinner, I pushed the lamb chops and baked potato and stringbeans-with-mushrooms around on my plate endlessly rearranging the food.

"No, thank you, Mom," I kept saying. "No, thank you. I'm just not hungry. I can't eat a thing." My plan was to hold out as long as I could, so she'd see I meant it, and then tell her what was going on. We'd talk, and then maybe she'd listen to me.

She began to suggest alternatives. The refrigerator was full. I could have anything I liked. Anything.

"I'm just not hungry, Mom," I repeated. "I don't have any appetite tonight."

"How about supper at Burger King?" she suggested. This from the woman who put down all fast foods? It showed her desperation.

"No thank you, Mom." The chance of a lifetime—lost.

Again the thermometer said I was normal.

Off she went to the drugstore for a digital thermometer that she put under my arm. It registered exactly the same: 98.6.

I couldn't get the Tarheel off my mind. Felicia was right; if he'd been real mean, I could've ended up bald. But why did he hate me? I didn't do anything to him.

Frantic was the word for Mom when I still wasn't hungry next morning. She was at the phone. "I'm going to call your father."

"Why? So he can worry all the way across the country? I'm telling you, I'm not sick. Besides it's five o'clock in the morning there."

She put down the phone. *AND SHE DIDN'T BRING UP THE TRAY!* First time! Progress. However, she continued to try to coax me and tempt me. This time my mouth was sealed tighter than a bank vault.

"I'm feeling fine," I insisted. "I've just lost my appetite. It happens to kids in school all the time."

A major lie.

I was aching for food. Itching for it. Yearning, longing, dying for food. Indeed, I had not lost my appetite. It was there inside me, a wolf in my belly gnawing, continually gnawing.

"Really, Mom. I'm just not in the mood to eat."

My mother was a lot more than frantic.

In class, I ignored the bully behind me. Sitting with

my shoulders hunched high, I pretended he didn't exist till late in the afternoon when I had a strange experience. I heard my own words echoed in a whisper. Not exactly my own words; Lincoln's words. Was I imagining it?

I looked back, but he was just writing in his notebook. I felt spooked. Then I heard it again, not a hallucination but a whisper from behind, ever so faint, "So you're the little woman who started this great war."

I turned around in my seat. "Yes, I am," I declared loudly. Miss Kahn looked up. "Asa?"

"Sorry, just thinking out loud." I felt myself blushing.

I had never declared war before.

For two-and-a-half-days I managed without one bite of food. Awesome—because I was truly starving. And I didn't cheat.

Felicia was dazzled.

I felt more grown up every hour that passed. If Gandhi, a very old frail man could do it, I knew I could, too. I did drink lots of water to fill myself up. My insides gurgled like a brook. And the wolf inside me growled!

It was gross when my stomach talked in school. I

prayed the Tarheel wouldn't hear. He was struggling, trying to catch up in all the subjects. April is very late in the year to transfer to a new school.

Each time my stomach made noise, I looked at others meaningfully—my eyebrows slightly raised—as if the strange sounds were coming from them. Especially Sandra.

Or I began to hum to cover the agony of my suffering innards.

One night I had a weird dream: I was in a bakery surrounded by trays and trays of luscious eclairs, the soft shiny chocolate so delicious I could actually smell it. I had to sit down on the bakery floor on my hands to keep from stuffing my mouth. I woke up licking my lips and groaning.

On the third day of my fast, my petrified mother was sitting in the car outside the school building, waiting for me. Once she saw the full lunch bag, she wouldn't listen to any further arguments. "Get in the car," she said. "We're going to the doctor. Now."

I'd stalled too long.

"But Mom, I'm not sick. I'm just not hungry."

"Ever hear of anorexia?" she asked grimly. "Don't argue. Just get in the car."

"Mom, we don't need to go really. I'm not sick." I checked behind me to be sure no one else was near.

Discussing this through an open car-window had not been part of my plan. "To tell the truth, Mom, I'm on a hunger strike."

"A *what?*"

"A hunger strike."

"Asa, what are you saying? That's crazy."

I felt miserable trying to explain, but it needed to be said. "No it's not crazy. It's the truth! You feed me too much. I couldn't stop you any other way."

"I can't believe my ears—"

Just then Ramon and you-know-who and his cousin came running out of the schoolyard dribbling a basketball zig-zag back and forth among them. I dived into the car, and Mom took off like a race-car driver.

We didn't go to our family doctor. Oh, no! She took me to a shrink. A specialist in eating disorders. Which was odd because he was himself a very fat man, bald with a goatee.

A gray balloon with a beard. My heart sank at the sight of him.

He will never understand. He looks like he stuffs his face even more than I do—*did*—and he's happy. He'll think I'm dippy which is perfect for a shrink to think.

His name was Dr. Humboldt Hamburger, and he smiled when he said it. He could see his name was pretty funny. That was mildly hopeful.

First, he interviewed my mother privately in his office for a very long time. I could hear endless murmurs, his voice deep and hers soft, but not one clear word. My mother talked a lot.

When they came out, my mother's eyes were red and puffy, and she had to blow her nose.

I felt terrible. A million times worse than if she'd read my letter in Ann Landers's column. A trillion times worse! How could I do this to my pregnant mother? But what else could I do?

Gandhi was a genius! He waited till he was very old before he began fasting, so his mother was no longer around to worry about him. Millions of Indians worried and that way he changed history. A mother is something else.

"Your turn, Asa," Dr. Hamburger said, taking my hand to lead me into the office. His hand was as soft as marshmallows.

My mother took a step forward, as if she were coming, too, but she was not invited.

Together, we went into the sunny examination room with his nurse, and he gave me a thorough physical. He talked as he worked. "So you have stopped eating, Asa. Your mother tells me you are on a hunger strike. Reminds me of Mahatma Gandhi. Ever hear of him?"

I cleared my throat unable to answer.

He smiled. "I am a great admirer of *satyagraha*."

He was a smart man. Maybe he wouldn't think I was crazy.

"I understand you were tiny and had a hard time as an infant, and then asthma troubled you for many years. Mmm . . ." He listened through his stethoscope and wrote on a chart. Afterward, the nurse took blood and urine samples.

"We'll have to wait for the lab results," he said, once it was over and I was dressed, "but I don't see a thing wrong organically. No sign of those earlier troubles."

I was sitting on the round wooden chair beside his desk. "You seem fit as a fiddle to me."

A bass fiddle, I thought. Like, how can I tell you my troubles, *Dr. Blimpo?* You'll take what I say personally. How do you tell a fat doctor that being fat is ugly?

I shut my eyes and wished, and it happened. Just when everything seemed most hopeless. Just when the wolf in my belly was growling and tearing at me. The doctor got my message.

"You may have noticed that I am very large," he started, sitting back in his chair. "I have always been this way and cannot change it. My glands do not cooperate. That is probably what made me interested in eating disorders."

He smiled at me.

"Actually, I do not eat much, but whatever I eat stays with me. Or, rather, on me. So, since I cannot affect it, I do not let my size matter to me. And you must not let *my* size matter to you. You must speak to me honestly."

My cheeks burned again. "How . . . how did you know what I was thinking?"

"It is my business—my profession—to know. I also know that at this moment you are devastatingly hungry and eager to have the food I will prescribe. Right?" He smiled and his brown eyes actually twinkled!

I nodded, blinking back tears. *Food!* my mind screamed. *Food! Emergency rations! Send in the Red Cross!*

"Then I shall do just that. I shall not keep you here talking today, but you and your mother must return tomorrow, and perhaps again for several more visits at least. Till we've ironed out all of this."

Then he went out and talked to Mom privately and brought her back with him.

To me he said, "I have told your mother that I do not think you have a serious eating disorder."

To my mother he said, "She's hungry now. She will eat a light dinner tonight, and she must continue to eat *very* lightly. I will see you both again tomorrow."

"So soon?" my mother looked alarmed.

"I believe we can handle this quickly."

She nodded and turned to gaze at me for a second as if she didn't know who I was, and then she opened her arms and I moved into them. She hugged me and began to weep.

But not me. I was too happy for tears.

My terrible days of starvation were over! Food was in sight.

"I'm hungry, Mom," I said. "Let's go home."

"I'm so glad you're hungry. So glad! Nothing could make me happier." Immediately, she began to make plans. "I'm going to make you the most delicious dinner you ever—"

She was impossible to turn off. "Hold your courses, Mom," I said, looking to the doctor for help.

"Mmm. A light supper, Mrs. Andersen, as I suggested earlier. Nothing heavy on an empty stomach."

"Oh!" My mother's pale skin was pinker than a peony, she was so embarrassed. "What do you recommend?"

"Well, perhaps a poached egg and tea and toast, tonight."

"Of course, you're right. I'm just so happy Asa is not seriously sick."

"I can assure you she is not. But keep the meals very scanty."

"Is cold cereal okay for breakfast?" I asked the doctor.

"A hot meal is the way a child should begin the day," Mom protested.

"Cold cereal is acceptable, Mrs. Andersen. Everything in moderation. Let Asa decide what she wants to eat." He began to search around in his desk drawer. "Here's some reading matter on good eating, Asa. It will help you make good choices. You seem a sensible girl."

"Oh, she is," my mother said. "She's a wonderful girl."

I read the nutrition pamphlets carefully before I went to sleep. Proteins, fruits, and vegetables were the right stuff. "A piece of cake," I said to myself. Then, realizing that was the one thing that was not, I fell asleep laughing.

Next morning when I was hanging up my jacket in the wardrobe, Anita came along, and I whirled right around and hugged her, much to her surprise. "I love your report. So I made up a little poem in your honor, Anita. Listen:

'Gandhi

Is dandy.'"

I recited it merrily.

"*Gahndi*," Anita corrected me. "*Mahatma Gahndhi*. You must not think it rhymes with dandy." She looked troubled. "To me he is more than dandy. He is India's greatest hero. Mahatma means—"

"Great Soul. I won't ever forget. Haven't you heard of poetic license? If you're writing a poem, you can change pronunciation a bit, and spelling. And use words differently."

She did not look convinced.

I really owed her. I'd been thinking and thinking, trying to come up with a good way to repay her.

And I had one. "Anita, last night while I was in the shower, I thought up a great name for your father's new restaurant. A perfect name."

"Really?" Now her eyes were wide with curiosity.

"Yes. A New York name that's also Indian and tells where you're from. Imagine a sign in colored lights: *The New DELI!*"

"Oh, Asa!" Anita began to giggle. "It's a wonderful, Indian-New York name. I will tell my father." Giggling, she raised her hands palm-to-palm beneath her chin while tipping her head. "Thank you. You're very nice." She was still smiling as she headed toward her seat.

I had a new friend. That almost made up for Enemy Alien sitting behind me. My first thought had been that he was an extra-terrestrial. So he was, but the wrong kind. I would pay him back for the gum in my hair—in time.

In my lunch bag was a chicken and tomato sandwich on whole wheat bread and one big red Delicious apple. No sweets. Felicia and I had decided to bring the same lunch each day. She was willing to sacrifice dessert so I wouldn't have to suffer watching her eat it. *That's* a true friend. We'd also decided to coordinate what we wore.

Mom and I had an appointment to see Dr. Hamburger.

At last, I was on the long road that led to being slim.

5

Una Feliz Aurora!

A happy dawn. My Spanish was getting *bueno*. It wasn't school Spanish; it was grandma Spanish, the only way I could talk to Felicia's grandma. A happy dawn — Felicia's names were lovely.

What made this such a memorable day?

Numero Uno: My father was back with us.

Numero Dos: I got to realize my lifetime morning ambition.

I. My father, who'd come home in the middle of the night, woke me. Tiptoeing into my room, he whispered, "Good morning, Asa. Mom is resting. We talked till late and then the baby kicked a lot and kept her up."

Rubbing my eyes, I sat up. "I bet it's a boy. A girl would never make so much trouble."

"Your mother got a lot of kicks out of you," he teased,

"so watch those sexist remarks." Then, suddenly he was serious. "I understand that much happened in my absence."

"I'm sorry—" I began.

"No," he stopped me. "Don't apologize. We have to talk. Mom says to tell you to say good-bye to the tray. It's banished. From now on you eat breakfast with the grown-ups. So today let's, the two of us, get our own food, while she stays in bed."

"Okay!" I said.

"Can you pack your own lunch?"

"Sure. Felicia and I are bringing the same lunches, spaceman's sandwiches."

"Mmm?" He looked intrigued.

"*Star Kist* Tuna."

He groaned. "In that case, you'd better wear space sneakers. Nikes."

Too bad he didn't hang around because while I was putting on my slippers it occurred to me that astronauts could drink from the Big Dipper. But never from Black Holes.

In a flash I was washed, toothbrushed, combed, and into my jeans and navy, antique UNITED-FEDERATION-OF-PLANETS T-shirt. Felicia would be wearing the identical outfit, appropriate attire for eating our lunches.

I weighed myself; I'd lost three pounds. I smiled at my thinning image in the mirror, loving it.

Dr. Hamburger, if you weren't already married I'd ask you to wait for me. You're more beautiful than any skinny Tarheel. And there's so much of you.

Dr. Hamburger had killed THE TRAY!

He'd spent an hour with Mom and me yesterday, first in separate consultations and then together.

With me he had been very direct. "You are a beautiful girl. You are overweight. You are not sick. Outside is a devoted mother who feared when you were a baby that you would die, and then nursed you through many very hard years. She has developed a pattern of overfeeding you and overprotecting you. Am I correct?"

I nodded. "One hundred per cent. She stuffed me and stuffed me till you told her to stop." I would've felt like a rat for talking against her except he'd already figured it all out.

"Your mother loves you a great deal. If it's possible, perhaps too much."

I couldn't hold back the tears that began to trickle down my cheeks. "How can that happen? How can a mother be blind? I'm *too fat!* Anyone can see that."

Dr. Hamburger didn't shush me or tell me to stop.

He just brought out a box of tissues and waited till I quieted down.

Five tissues later he told me, "This is not a hard medical problem. We shall work it out together. You must be very gentle and kind with your mother—"

"—Because she's pregnant." I finished his sentence.

"Yes, and because she means well and loves you very much. Perhaps some day you'll understand better. But for now, we—you and I—have to help her to help herself.

"And you must learn some hard everyday words to use for the rest of your life. They are, 'No, thank you. I've had enough. No seconds. I do not want any more.'

"It will be particularly hard for you, at first. You will long for the sweets and the junk food, but you must learn to say no. Quietly. Don't draw attention to it. Just do it."

"Are you putting me on a diet, Doctor?"

"No, I decided against that." He smiled. "Grown-ups have always chosen what you ate. Now I'm going to leave it up to you. You only need to be sensible. I know you can do that."

Then he had a long talk with Mom while I looked at the pictures in magazines. The chimps were cute in *National Geographic*, but *VOGUE* had skeletal ladies in weird positions wearing bizarre dresses. Thin is nice but that was going too far.

Then we all consulted together. Mostly, he talked. "It will take you a while," he told Mom softly "to realize how much Asa needs you. What she doesn't need is all the food and fretting. She's the healthy child you always wanted her to be. Help her to eat a balanced diet."

He looked at her gravely. "And you and her father are as important to her as ever."

"When we came here," my mother complained, "my starving daughter was the patient. More and more I feel that I am the patient."

"We would have had your husband here, too, if he were around. It's a family problem. And you are well on the way to solving it."

We made arrangements; I would stop in once a week for the nurse to weigh me then he would see both of us in a month.

"And will that be the end of it?" Mom asked anxiously.

He shrugged. "With luck. And only if you bring that Danish recipe for baked herring. My wife is eager for it."

Oh no. She had told him about her hobby.

She promised not to forget.

Baked herring! I made a silent vow. There's one place I'm never going for dinner . . .

II. My lifetime morning ambition—*to sit at the round kitchen table eating cold cereal*—came true.

I set the table while Dad poured two glasses of orange juice from the container.

Dad had the kettle on while he spooned Earl Grey Tea into the china teapot. I went to work on my lunch. Too bad we had settled on tuna sandwiches today. Otherwise, with the whole refrigerator to myself there were endless oddball possibilities: chicken salad, bacon, and cheddar cheese, cold meatballs, and green peppers and onions.

My mouth watered just looking at the great food, and then I was immediately ashamed of myself. How could I be out of control so soon?

After spreading the tuna mixed with lemon juice on the bread, I tracked down lettuce and tomato and found a perfect apple (I hate brown spots!) and a can of cranberry juice. Cucumber slices instead of potato chips. Sensible? Dr. Hamburger would love it.

The kettle whistled, and, carefully, Dad poured the boiling water into the teapot. I was so glad to have him home again; Mr. Principal in his white shirt, jazzy red tie, navy jacket, the works.

He looks classy, I thought; classy is the right word for a principal. The bright tie, however, was not a principal's tie. It had pizzazz. My mother's word. I smiled at my classy, pizzazzy father.

He filled his cup. He was a tea addict. He claimed he couldn't start his day without it. He liked it impossibly hot. In fact, he began to sip immediately.

"My dear," he said quietly, "Mom told me you went on a hunger strike while I was gone. Tell me about it."

So I told him about everything, including Ann Landers and Gandhi and Dr. Hamburger, and he listened attentively. "Mom takes *too* good care of me," I concluded.

"In all my years as a principal," he marveled, "I never heard that complaint about a mother before."

"I'm too fat."

Raising a hand to quiet my protest, he continued, "But your mother is pregnant, Asa, and she's not having an easy time."

"I know, Daddy, and I'm really sorry I worried her, but I didn't know what else to do. I tried so many times to tell her—and you—but no one wanted to listen."

Again he sat silent, lost in thought. Till he said, "It's all right. You did nothing wrong. I guess I've been so busy trying to be a good principal I stopped noticing the really important things going on in my family."

"Daddy—"

"Let me finish, please. You're a lovely girl, Asa, but you'll be even lovelier when you're slim and happy.

And you *are* old enough to start making decisions for yourself. With good backup advice, of course."

He was sad. "We just hadn't noticed how quickly you were growing up. But you are going to be an older sibling soon, and that's a really major job. Okay, go ahead, your turn to talk."

"Thanks," I began, then I just shook my head "— Daddy." I was so grateful that I had no words for once. None. All I could think of to say was, "Cold cereal and banana? I got Mom to let me try *Cap'n Krunch*. It's not diet food, but I wanted to try it—just once."

"No, thank you. Not for me. I'd die of sugar overdose. That stuff is a cereal killer. I'll have *Fruit 'n Fibre*."

"Yuck." I passed that box down to him.

"Yuck? A Tibetan animal?" he guessed. He aimed the stream of little bits of cardboardy cereal into his bowl. "A wild ox?"

"Not *yak*, Daddy. Your cereal deserves a loud *yuck*."

Watching, I wondered why so many of the foods that were good for you had to look as if they'd been recycled. Fibre was to stuff a pillow with, not to *eat*. I wouldn't feed a monkey fibre and no smart monkey would touch it. He'd choose bananas any day and he'd be so right.

"Yuck is a perfectly good word," I handed my father the sharp knife and a banana, "like *Ugh!* and *Phew!*"

He raised his eyebrows, and as he refilled his cup, he said quite seriously, "Let's see—*Yuck* and *Ugh* and *Phew*."

It made me giggle to hear him. The sounds were sticky in his mouth, just not right for a principal or even for a grown-up.

He weighed each one on his tongue. "Fair enough. They're sounds that express feeling. But I wouldn't go so far as to call them perfectly good words."

He chewed his mouthful of nutritious, shredded blotter. Then he drained his teacup, set it on the saucer, and lifted the teapot lid to look inside.

"Ah, terrific!" He poured himself a third cup. "I was afraid that all that was left were the lees."

"*Lees?*" The word was a gunshot in my ears.

"Yes, you know, the sediment. The bitter stuff at the bottom."

"Aah," I said and stored up that verbal ammunition to be used against the enemy.

My father looked at his watch. "Sorry, dear. I must run. I've been away and there's much to do." He carried his dishes to the sink.

"I'll wash up. It'll only take a sec."

"Thanks, Asa. I'll get my briefcase and take off."

He came over and kissed me on the cheek. "It's good to be home," he said, and two minutes later I heard the front door quietly close.

I washed up quickly then set off myself. I never drove to school with him; the less attention I called to being his daughter the better. My first stop was Felicia's house, and while I walked I practiced my grandma Spanish.

Felicia's grandmother was a friendly, small, old lady, olive-skinned, with a very wrinkled face and a cloud of the softest white hair crowning her head. To her, Spanish was a treasure, the great language of the world. She spoke Spanish to everyone expecting them to understand. Even me. Always.

She answered the door. "*Buenos días,*" I said, and for that I got a gigantic hug.

"*Buenos días,* Asa." Her face was one big smile. Then the questions began: How was I, and how was my mother with the *bebé*, and how was my father, *el principal?*

I managed to answer. (Two words repeated did it. *Muy bien.* As long as my family stayed healthy, *Abuelita* and I could hold conversations.)

Felicia came tearing through the hall, gave her grandmother a quick squeeze, grabbed her bookbag, and we were off.

"Remember what I told you," she said. "Don't let him bully you. If he starts anything, then you have to attack."

"What does that mean, Felicia? Attack how?"

"My father always says bullies are surprised when

you fight back. So, surprise him. Fight back in your own way. It'll come to you."

I thought about it off and on all during the busy school day, but I had my doubts. What would come to me?

After phys. ed. where I flew on the rings and glided down the ropes, I had an arithmetic quiz which I didn't fly and glide through. I stumbled through it, and only managed to pass because I recalled two examples from drills earlier in the week. Arithmetic was my most un-favorite subject.

Otherwise, it continued to be a particularly nice day because Monster Boy left me alone. Why? An unde-clared truce?

Maybe he's found someone else to bother, I thought. Someone he hates worse than me. I was really hopeful.

I wondered if it was another girl. And if so, who? till just at dismissal time, as we assembled and were crowded next to each other along the back of the room, waiting to begin to file out.

Then I heard the whisper again. "Only crazy Yan-kees would name a girl Asa." This was followed by a nasty little singsong verse.

> *Asa Hearts,*
> *Asa Clubs,*
> *Asa Diamonds,*
> *Asa Spades.*

My Dante had made me a poem—a lousy one!

My classmates ahead of me had just begun moving out of the room and were already slowly snaking toward the stairs. The line suddenly halted in the hallway because of a crowd of other classes backed up at the stairwell.

I turned around and faced him. "Do you know what *lees* are? Do you know where the word comes from? It means soggy, drippy leftovers after you soak something. That's what *Lees* are—you and all your relatives."

"You're crazy," he said.

"Look it up, Tarheel!"

I turned back to follow the kids along the corridor, but I was steaming mad, and I didn't step forward the way I normally would have. Instead, I dragged my right foot behind me.

It connected.

He tripped and stumbled, off balance for a step or two, but, to my great disappointment, he managed to straighten himself and didn't fall flat on his face.

Felicia, luckily, at that moment, glanced back trying to see where I was. She saw the legwork, the connection, and the stumble. She put both thumbs up and grinned.

Felicia was right. *Attack* was the only way. He'd minded what I said about his name. And he hated that I tripped him.

"Watch your feet," he muttered, his face red and his dark eyes burning, "Fatso!"

The name stung me like acid. For a second or two my eyes were blurry with tears, then I brushed them aside furiously. I tried to hurry down the stairs. I had to get away both from the name and the name caller. He might even say it again. He might say it loud. "*FATSO!*" I hated the word. I hated *him*.

My mind was a tumult as I went along toward home, thoughts surging back and forth: He had to remember, for a whole weekend, that I wasn't just a patsy. He would remember the stumble and the meaning of the word *Lees*.

I, on the other hand, had two days to celebrate that I'd struck back. And to plan future defenses.

Still, on the other hand, he'd trashed me, too, painfully.

In that round, he came out ahead.

I tried to put "Fatso," out of my head. I kept telling myself that I had put him down and that was what counted. But "Fatso" was lodged in my brain like a permanent echo. It wouldn't go away.

My mom, without knowing anything about anything, saved my life. Really. On Saturday afternoon, she said. "Let's go to the mall for a little while." She tired easily so it would be a quick trip. "I need several things, and, who knows, we might see something nice for you."

I have never been known to turn down such an offer.

"Would you like a training bra?" she asked me, in the car, as if it were some unimportant piece of clothing like a handkerchief.

"If you think I need it, Mom."

"Your body is beginning to change as you thin down. If you don't need the bra right now then you will very soon. You're going to have a lovely figure. Definitely."

We had a nice afternoon together. I got two new tee shirts and a pair of jeans one size smaller than I'd been wearing. They were a little snug but I'd shrink into them very soon. And I also became the proud owner of one peach and one rainbow bra. Both satin.

What a beautiful word *definitely* is!

6

Ingrids 13, Asas 0

Sunday morning we went to church as usual. I was particularly glad to go because the scale said I'd lost nearly eight (*ocho!*) pounds. I knew I had to offer thanks.

It was a clear, beautiful spring day; nobody could be gloomy with the gleaming sun pouring through the stained glass windows making the whole inside of the church iridescent. I felt as if I'd stepped into the middle of a rainbow.

I loved the music and the quiet caring order of the service though I could have done without the very long sermon and all the announcements. Reverend Peterson sure liked to talk a lot. Often when he said something, he repeated it several different ways. I guess he wanted to be sure we got it.

Usually—afterwards—while my parents chatted with old friends, I hurried outside to walk around because I'd been sitting for so long. The freedom of the gardens was wonderful especially on the Sundays that Pastor Peterson got carried away with parables and examples that reminded him of MORE EXAMPLES. While he was speaking all the unreachable unscratchable parts of me—like the small of my back and the soles of my feet—began to itch, and I knew better than to start fidgeting in the pew. I loved the moment of release.

But there was no scooting outside for me on this particular Sunday. I had a mission, a major project; like my parents I, too, was into Scandinavian research. Personal Scandinavian research. Much more important than herring recipes. In my pocket I carried a pencil and my small assignment pad.

Moving rapidly toward the vestibule without actually running, I was first to reach the great wooden doors where Pastor Peterson always placed himself after services—his receiving line—as he greeted the congregants. I quickly stationed myself out of sight by slipping unseen into the dark shadow behind the one opened door. There I waited quietly.

Our small neighborhood church was one where everyone knew one another and used first names. That was perfect for me; I needed to hear the pastor greeting the women.

I needed to hear all their first names!

"Good morning," Pastor Peterson beamed at each parishioner. Then he shook hands vigorously and followed that up by asking, "How are you?"

The majority of the older folks must have thought that what he really wanted most in this world was a detailed up-to-the-minute medical report, so that's what they gave him: long descriptions of flu and arthritis, diabetes and broken bones, and a lot of stuff I never heard of.

He got bulletins on the latest pills and the best and worst doctors. He (and I) learned all about one severe antibiotic reaction: itching, swelling, nausea, the works.

I had no idea that that many things could go wrong with people's bodies. Particularly since these folks were all looking so nice dressed up in spring suits and shirts and ties and hats with flowers. The line crawled along because the pastor listened most politely and comforted and cheered *each* person he spoke to. He even spent ten minutes mourning a cat that had run off.

After the first few people, I paid attention only to each woman's name, writing it down on my pad immediately. Then I tuned out the rest of the conversation. Eavesdropping is not polite; I only wanted to hear the names.

Later I sat down on an old stone bench in the church garden and tallied up my findings: two Berthas, three Heddas, four Sigrids, five Astrids, and thirteen Ingrids along with the many normal Marys and Lauras and Joans.

Final score: Ingrids 13, Asas 0.

Not one Asa in the pack, to say nothing of Alfifa, which is what farmers feed to horses.

I was disappointed, but not surprised.

Then it was time to go. I put it to my father immediately. "Dad, I heard Reverend Peterson greeting all the ladies after church, and there wasn't *one* Asa." (I didn't even mention Alfifa. I had *known* that one wouldn't occur!)

"How come no one—not even the two old ladies who used walkers—has my name if it's such a wonderful ancient name? How come there were *thirteen* Ingrids? I wouldn't mind being an Ingrid."

"What? What's this all about?" my mother wondered.

"Asa thinks her name is strange. Remember, Asa, 'That which we call a rose—'"

"'—By any other name would smell as sweet.'" He had used that line many times. "Juliet."

He nodded approvingly. He was driving in after-church traffic, so he had to pay close attention to the road.

All the Berthas and Heddas and Sigrids and Astrids and, especially, the Ingrids—or their husbands—were driving home, too, and they were dangerous drivers. He had to thread his way past tricky *slow* drivers. Stop-shorters. Lane-changers. No-signallers. And horn-blowers.

"Asa is a beautiful name," my mother said. "Both your names are especially chosen. Dad and I spent months thinking about them. And then a lot more time reading history."

History! Come on. I shuddered. Where did they get their zonko ideas? "How come there are so many Ingrids, Mom?"

My mother smiled. "Because the beautiful movie actress, Ingrid Bergman, was popular when these women were born. Maybe Daddy will stop at the video store on our way home and pick up the movie, *Casablanca*. She's gorgeous in it and we can watch it tonight. It's wonderful."

"Play it again, Sam," my father said mysteriously. I looked around. There wasn't a Sam in sight. And then he began to sing—and my mother's fingers began to play on an invisible keyboard atop the dashboard as she joined in, humming.

I couldn't believe what I was seeing and hearing. My own father swaying his head and crooning.

Occasionally he forgot he was a principal, and my mother forgot she was a grown-up, and they acted silly. Rarely, but it did happen. Those wonderful moments hadn't occurred often during the last months, so I wasn't sorry it was going on.

"Would you mind telling me what you are doing, Mom?"

"I'm playing 'As Time Goes By' on an air piano."

She kept right on moving her fingers, looking really happy.

I was glad—but even gladder that the car windows were practically all shut up. I wished our car had tinted windows like limos do. I loved that my parents were silly and fooling around, but I wanted it to be happening in private. At home.

With these parents, it was not at all surprising I got named for a dinosaur queen.

They went on singing snatches of this goopy love song and trying to remember the words and humming what they didn't know till my father pulled up at the video store and took off his seat belt.

I wouldn't let it rest. Research!

They hadn't really answered my question. "I still don't understand. Why isn't anyone besides me named Asa?"

"You tell her about her namesake, Nora," my father said, "while I see if I can rent the film." He got out.

"Asa is a very ancient, distinguished name," my mother began, willingly.

I wasn't buying it. "It doesn't sound distinguished. Elizabeth and Victoria *sound* distinguished. They're long complicated names. Asa sounds more like a bandage. Anyway, *who* was she? *What* did she ever do?"

"Asa was a great queen, very brave and honorable. An evil king, Gudrod, wanted to marry her, but was refused. He murdered her father and brother and carried her off along with a lot of treasure. She had no choice but to live with him, and she did, unhappily, for many years. He treated her abominably. Her reputation for wisdom and generosity was known throughout the kingdom.

"One night when King Gudrod was very drunk, he was mysteriously speared to death. The suspicion was that Asa's servant had done it. Gudrod's heirs—sons by a former wife—never blamed her or made a move against her because she was a good woman and their father had led her a terrible life. They didn't accuse her nor did she ever deny it.

"She was a brave and virtuous lady and was treated with honor and respect by all until her death."

"How did you find all this out?"

"Well, there are various old histories and legends. But, more than that, there's Queen Asa's ship—that she was buried in."

"She got buried in a *ship?*"

"Yes," my mother said, "but not at sea. They were a seagoing people, so they used ships as tombs—on land."

Weirder and weirder.

"It was the custom in those days to bury royalty with all their household possessions and riches for use in the next life. So the Queen was surrounded by furniture, clothing, carpets—"

"Ten centuries old?" The musty idea made me screw up my nose.

"More," said my mother. "The ship was discovered and excavated in 1904. No one knew about it before then."

"Where did they find it?"

"In Oseberg, Norway. Preserved under layers of blue clay and peat—a kind of earth. The ship has incredible woodcarvings and treasures on it. She must have been *some* queen."

"Where is all this stuff now?"

"It's in a museum in Oslo. One day perhaps we can go and see it—"

Actually, I thought, that might be fun. And I know

someone who ought to be forced to come along, so he could learn all about it.

I actually was beginning to enjoy the story. The more I thought about the good queen and the wicked Gudrod, the better I liked it.

Did I dare ask about Alfifa? Did I really want to hear?

I might as well know the worst.

"And who was Alfifa?"

"Another great queen, the mother of King Harald of England, and a strong and ambitious woman. When I first heard the name, I loved the sound of it. It's so musical. Just listen to your names," my mother said fondly. "Asa Alfifa Andersen. They're so alliterative."

I would never never never in a trillion years agree about Alfifa. NEVER.

But the name Asa? How many kids have ten centuries of history behind their names? It was something to be proud of.

When we got home, I dashed to phone Felicia. Just my luck she was out babysitting. I tried again in a few minutes, and her father said she wouldn't be back till late evening. I'd just have to wait.

So we had our Sunday dinner and then settled down around the TV set and watched *Casablanca*. There was no question about Ingrid Bergman being very beautiful. Her cheekbones were to die for. My parents really melted over the story, but personally, I didn't think it was so hot.

I mean—this couple were caught in Casablanca during the war? And she fell in love with a funny-looking guy who owned a nightclub called "Rick's"? 'Cause his name was Rick. So the problem was, should she hang out in Africa with Rick or go back into danger with her brave husband?

I liked her husband a lot. He was cool.

Anyway, these characters were pretty old to be having all these romantic problems. You ought to know who you love by the time you're *that* old. I will. But the movie kept my attention, so I guess it was okay.

Afterward, I got Felicia on the phone and she was really into my news about my name.

"Did I say they *dug* my first name up? Wrong word. They excavated it—

"From a boat. A buried boat—

"No, not under water. It was buried on land under a whole bunch of blue clay and peat—that's a kind of earth—

"I am not bonkers. I'm telling you what my mother told me. These people used ship-tombs on land—"

For once, Felicia stopped interrupting and listened. She was so quiet, I thought we were disconnected. "Felicia?" I called. "You there?"

"Still here. That's really really a great story. So—"

she paused, "now I guess you know what you've got to do, Asa?"

"I certainly do," I said, standing on my toes, straight and tall, pushing out my bosom a bit—I was definitely getting a bosom—and looking at myself in the mirror.

Someday soon I knew that I would look into the mirror and see a long lean blonde gazing back at me. Not one of those *VOGUE* skinnys. This blonde would have bright, sexy eyes and beautiful skin, and her loose soft hair would glide about her face softly first on one side, then the other like it does in shampoo ads.

She might slightly resemble Ingrid Bergman. The cheekbones, particularly.

Someday soon those sleeping Viking genes my mother was always going on about would suddenly wake up, and then there would be no stopping me.

Perhaps I, too, would become a movie star and all over the world little girls would be named for me. No more Ingrids. That would be old-fashioned. *Asa* would be on everyone's lips. Crowds of Asas. Mobs!

Tarheels would have to stuff their ears with cotton, so they wouldn't be deafened by crowds cheering, "Asa!"

I would sign autographs for everyone who asked, no matter how tired my hands got. A movie queen should be gracious. Of course, I'd give away pictures of myself.

And, in TV and live interviews, I would tell the story of Queen Asa and the wicked Gudrod so that the entire world might know the history of that illustrious name.

It was a story well worth the telling. And well worth hearing.

"I know exactly what I have to do," I said resolutely. "Tomorrow, I have to take out Robert Edward Lee."

"*Sí,*" Felicia agreed.

"Robert Edward *Gudrod* Lee!"

"*Sí, sí, sí!*"

7

Neh, Neh, Neh

I planned to zap the creep the next morning. I had my own strategy. I'd just brush my teeth, dress, wash and comb, have my breakfast, and then I'd go to school and quietly wipe him out.

My Viking genes would stand me in good stead. He would be: pulverized. Squashed. Wasted. I might not be able to *knock* him down, but surely I was smart enough to *cut* him down to size.

About as big as an ant was the right size for him. Or a bacterium? Or a molecule? Or an atom?

I come from ancestors who were smart enough to bury precious treasures—like my namesake's jewelry, household goods, and wood-carvings—so that a thousand years later they would still be beautiful.

Smart enough in the very early days of civilization to

discover the blue clay that preserves perishables and to use it appropriately.

Let him start up with me. Oh, yes, just let him start. Maybe I could carry in a bunch of soggy tea leaves and put them on his desk! But how would I ever explain to my parents why I was emptying the bottom of the teapot into a baggie and carrying it away?

I'd have to think of a reason. It was really a superior idea, to come into the classroom and set this little mushy gift down—maybe with a pinhole or two in the plastic so it would drip a bit onto his desk. I'd simply say, "See—*Lees.*"

Actually, all my blue jeans were Lees because those fit me best. And I could name a whole bunch of good Lees: Annabel in the poem by Poe, and the Lee who signed the Declaration of Independence and the actor, Bruce Lee. I wasn't being quite fair, but I didn't care about being fair.

Who was he to make fun of anyone else's name? I would cancel him like a stamp.

He was *so* proud of where he came from: the tobacco state. My parents didn't smoke or let anyone smoke in our home, so I know all about the dangers of tobacco. His hometown, Winston-Salem, was Cigaretteville, USA.

I thought of other damages to inflict on His Royal

Obnoxiousness: glue on his seat or Dubble Bubble—a taste of his own medicine—but those would cause only minor discomfort.

I needed to execute a major strike.

I could arrange for his various possessions to disappear: his pen and pencils, so he couldn't do his writing exercises; his assignment book, on a day when there was a ton of note taking and homework; his lunch, his library books.

Yes, he'd found the library; someone else must have told him where it was because he was reading *Twenty Thousand Leagues Under the Sea*; he carried the book around with him. I had read it and loved it. If we were friends, we might have talked about it . . .

But he was no friend. He was *The Enemy!* He had to lose something he valued. That would teach him a lesson.

Wilder ideas occurred to me. It would be wonderful if I could steal his pants during phys. ed. so he'd have to walk around all day in maroon gym shorts (well, maybe it wouldn't be so effective because he'd look terrific; lots of girls would love him in shorts). Anyway, I wouldn't ever go near the boys' locker room, so I junked that idea.

One thing for sure: Miss Kahn would never suspect me. *My* father was principal, and I had never been in serious trouble at school. The setup was perfect.

So many criminal fantasies leaped into my mind and had to be suppressed, I was truly amazed. I'd thought I was a pretty nice person, but I was brimming with anger and the desire for revenge.

If hiding something he treasured didn't work out, I just might spread the word that a certain girl had a crush on him and they were going out. Sandra White leapt into my mind.

Twice in the past week, Sandra had dallied at the lunch counter waiting, and then carried her tray to the table where Robert was eating, even though he and Ramon and Tommy were busy looking at baseball cards and never even noticed her.

Yes, Sandra White would do.

Rumors—gossip—could have the lunchroom buzzing. *Why* had he transferred in midyear? He must have done something awful down among the Tarheels.

Maybe he got into a fight and hurt a kid. Or bit a teacher?

Naah, he was very polite to Miss Kahn. He even called her "Ma'am." But he was probably in disgrace for some awful thing he'd done. No doubt he'd been expelled. For what? If only I could find out.

My head filled with delirious scenarios and more practical plans, I went to bed. Felicia and I would work out tactics, and then the real war would begin. When I finished with him, the bully would be on his knees begging for mercy. I could see him now. Crawling.

"Oh, please forgive me, Asa. Please. I'm so sorry. I promise it will never, never happen again. How can I make it up to you? Please!" Those large dark eyes would be burning with humility and sincerity.

How proud Felicia would be of me for fighting back. Felicia hated bullies. She gloried in her initials: F-E-A-R, and she took pleasure in the fact that Puerto Ricans were an extremely proud people who never lost their pride.

The walk was taking too long. I was so eager to get Felicia to help plan my foe's downfall that I ran the last block and arrived breathless. Felicia's grandmother, answering the door, drew back a step and put her hand to her throat when she saw me arrive, panting.

"*Buenos días,*" I gasped.

Mrs. Rodriguez insisted I sit on the stool near the door, where people usually sat to take boots on and off. She began to talk. Her Spanish was rapid because she was alarmed by my haste. I could not follow her at all.

So I mumbled my usual *muy biens* in answer to the questions. I could see real concern—or fright—in the old woman's brown eyes as she inspected me.

Felicia came swirling through the long front hall like a cyclone, but her grandmother grabbed her arm, and, talking fast, blocked the front door.

Surprised, Felicia translated. "*Abuelita* wants to know if there's trouble at home. Are your mother's legs swollen? And does the baby move? She says you ran all the way here, so she's worried. She had eleven children and some were hard to carry, so she understands."

"I only ran so I could get here to talk to you faster," I said. "About you-know-who."

Felicia rolled her eyes.

"Tell your grandmother my mother's legs are normal. She just needs to rest a lot, so she's taking it easy. But the baby kicks really hard. I felt it. That baby moves all the time."

Felicia gave her the message, rapid-fire.

As she talked, her grandmother relaxed and actually rubbed her own belly and smiled. It was almost as if she was waiting for the news that the baby was kicking and moving. She offered a torrent of excited Spanish.

"We'll be late, Felicia," I warned.

"I know. *Abuelita* says a baby who kicks a lot is all right." Felicia kissed her grandmother and told her, "*Tarde! Tarde!*" and off we hurried.

"If he teases me today, I'm going to nail him, Felicia."

"Right. But how?"

As we walked along, I reviewed the various schemes I'd thought of. Felicia listened intently.

"I think the idea of getting hold of something he really cares about is the way," she said. "Make him beg."

That appealed to me. "Yes," I agreed. "Oh, yes!"

"All we have to do is figure out what he values most."

We went along in deep thought.

Throughout history the power of concentration has led to great breakthroughs: using fire; inventing the wheel; discovering vaccines; understanding evolution; smashing the atom; escaping gravity. Just so are ideas born—and one came to me.

"I've got it," I said, and I actually jumped for joy. "*I* have got it!"

"What?"

"He has dozens of baseball cards. And the best ones are in an album. Each card is in a plastic sleeve, and when he brings the album he carries it in a special box, and he doesn't let anyone hold it. I saw him wash his hands after lunch and then sit down with Ramon, holding the album and turning the page himself—like each one was made of gold. They trade cards, only Ramon carries his cards in a shoebox. Robert loves his album."

"Sounds good," Felicia said. "I hope he brings it to-day."

"Amen!" I said fervently.

And so, when I took my seat and noted the album carefully placed along the top of his desk, I began to breathe faster. My face grew warm. I only hoped the back of my neck, which he could see, wasn't flushed with excitement.

The treasure was there all right, but how to get it? He didn't trust it out of his sight for a second.

The day passed uneventfully. I could not concentrate on anything except that album. I was so excited I misspelled *emancipator* and *secession*, two words on the social studies list that I had practiced and knew perfectly well.

Lunchtime was coming. That might be Robert Lee's *moment of truth*. That's my father's favorite way to describe a time when reality smacks you in the face.

I arrived in the lunchroom very early and sat on a bench, my lunch on the table before me, my books piled beside me to save a place for Felicia.

He was sitting several tables away. I didn't see the album. Sandra White was already perched right there beside him; that girl didn't give up.

There was no way, no way, I could make off with his album. Even though I ached for it to happen, reality wasn't going to smack Robert Edward Lee in the face that lunch hour. Too bad.

Afterward, I didn't even remember what I ate. I didn't even long for dessert and then stop myself by thinking the magic words, "Gandhi is Dandy." I couldn't focus on anything except revenge. It had become a complete hang-up; an obsession.

At three, we lined up to go home. He was right behind me, as usual, and he didn't say anything till we were almost down on the ground floor.

Then, on the second floor stairwell as the line bunched up to let the classes before us pass, he crowded me and I heard his mocking whisper in my ear once again.

> *Asa Hearts*
> *Asa Clubs,*
> *Asa Spades,*
> *Asa Diamonds.*

I braced myself.

And, again. "Asa Hearts . . ." He added a gravelly finale, "Neh, neh, neh!"

The line started moving down the stairs. It was too dangerous to act then.

I held back all the way down to the ground floor

gym; Felicia was already outside, and the place was empty since we were last on the line. It is possible that I would have chickened out, that I wouldn't have had the nerve to carry out my plan then—*if* he hadn't added the *neh, neh, neh*.

But that was too much.

I swung around and made a flying grab for the plastic treasure box in his right hand. He was holding it firmly, but he was so surprised by the attack, I wrested it from him on the very first pull and moved off with it.

"Hey!" he said, "Asahead—hand it over!"

But I was already backing away from him fast. I didn't know what I'd do with the album, but he wasn't going to get it back. I'd die first.

What a headline that would make in the *Daily News*:

"Sixth Grader Killed Over Baseball Card Album: Another Peculiar Crime in the New York City Schools." And the *Post* would run a huge picture of me with the caption: *"Asa Andersen, Innocent Victim of School Violence."* (I hoped the name Alfifa would not appear.)

My feet moved swiftly.

If only Felicia would have the sense to come looking for me. Then the two of us could toss the album back and forth the way the boys tossed the basketball in the school playground.

Come on, Felicia, I willed, silently, *Come on back! I need help, Felicia. I need help now. If you don't come back I'll never forgive you!*

"Give it here! It's mine!" he said, advancing.

"No," I said, dropping the cover on a bench as I passed. "Never!"

He bent his knees and reached for the cover, not taking his eyes off me. I lifted the album out of the bottom half of the box and dropped that on the floor. When he bent again to pick it up, I widened the distance between us.

I was close to the drinking fountain now, very close.

And I realized exactly what I was going to do.

So did he.

He froze in place. "No!" he said. "It's valuable."

Now we'd both stopped moving.

"Too bad."

"It belongs to me. You have to respect people's property."

"My name belongs to me. It's more valuable than any stupid album. Asa was a queen a thousand years ago."

"Who says? I never heard of her."

"History says. They still have the stuff from her tomb."

He shrugged. "So what? What was so special about her?"

"Plenty."

"Tell me one special thing if you know so much."

"A wicked king named Gudron forced her to marry him."

He scoffed. "That's not so special."

The enemy was beginning to edge toward me in very slow motion. He was keeping me talking to throw me off guard.

"She managed to destroy Gudron in the end," I went on, watching him warily. "Her servant speared him to death. That's the kind of dangerous queen Asa was— and I've got her name!"

Now he crouched, silent, bouncing on the balls of his feet, about to lunge for the book.

"Don't!" I warned, and I turned and held the album high over the drinking-spout, my foot on the pedal. "I'll soak it unless you apologize for calling me Fatso and promise never to say that or my name again as long as you live." My whole body was trembling.

"You wouldn't dare wet it." He looked scared. "I'll report you to the principal."

"He's my father. You think he'd believe *you?* You just came here a little while ago."

"That's not fair."

"Fair?" My voice cracked. "You think gum is fair? You think what you've been doing is fair?"

I pressed the pedal—but I couldn't bear to soak the album. I just couldn't. So my toes were light on the pedal and I held the book high up, and only a thin spray lightly squirted one corner.

"I apologize—"

"For?"

"I apologize for calling you Fatso."

"And?"

"I promise I won't say your name ever again." He talked very fast. "I swear! You'll ruin my cards. My best cards are in there—the Babe Ruth I only just bought!"

There was agony in his voice.

I couldn't resist. "Neh, neh, neh!" I said, and I threw the album back at him.

Then I turned away, and, straight and tall, walked with all the dignity I could manage across the gym and out the door to where Felicia was waiting on the steps.

Felicia's face was one huge smile.

"Why didn't you come back in and help me?" I asked.

"I figured you could handle him."

I forgave her.

Felicia couldn't stop praising my smarts. "He won't bother you again," she promised.

I had peculiar mixed feelings. I was glad I'd stood up for myself. Yet, I didn't feel as good about it as I'd expected. I hoped I didn't ruin the book or any of the cards. Especially the Babe Ruth card.

He was mean and a tease, but if that's what I had to become to outwit him then was I any better? I didn't want to be like that.

If only he'd behaved differently, we could have been friends. If only I'd been named Mary or Jane or Sue. If only . . . The best-looking boy in the school was now my enemy. Forever!

"I have to stop at the doctor's and get weighed," I said.

"You're looking skinny."

"Eight pounds off if my scale is not lying."

We hugged. "From now on, sixth grade is going to be *el paraíso,*" Felicia promised, as I moved on to the corner. "I can see the future like a fortune-teller," she called after me. "Tomorrow will be a day of peace."

But it sometimes happens that fortune-tellers—even the very best crackerjack seers into the future—have occasional off-days.

8

History Repeats Itself

Eight pounds; Dr. Hamburger's scale agreed with ours for once.

"You're going to be a sylph," the nurse said.

"What's that?"

She lent me her paperback dictionary: *a dainty imaginary being who inhabits the air.*

"Thank you." I sped home happily, my braid swinging merrily behind me thumping against my bookbag. All the sacrifices: potato chips, peanuts, candy bars and eclairs, all the seconds of every food I loved and had gone without paid off. I moved fast but was mindful not to step on any cracks—though I'm not superstitious.

I just skimmed along, practically airborne, confident that I could handle whatever came. Sixth grade would be a pleasure from now on. Felicia had to be right. I could hardly wait for the next morning.

But I never made it to school next morning, and I didn't even remember to phone Felicia. She and her grandmother were worried sick when I didn't show up or call. This had never happened before.

The night had been a strange one. Another weird dream. This time I was sitting on my favorite stone bench in the churchyard, and an ugly freckled frog hopped into my lap. I petted him and fed him a *krumkaker* I had in my pocket. The frog gobbled it up, and then—*wham!*—a flash of lightning and a masked young prince kneeled before me, kissing my hand.

Just as he was about to unmask, I was awakened. My mother's voice. It was 2:14, the numbers gleaming at me in the absolute darkness. I stumbled out of bed, and in the hallway met my father coming to get me.

"Mom has gone into labor," he said.

That was dangerous. "It's much too soon, isn't it, Daddy?"

"I'm afraid so."

"How much too soon?"

"Ten weeks, Asa. Can you get into your clothes quickly? The ambulance is on its way. We'll go along to the hospital." He left me in the blackness.

"Just like when I was born," I whispered to the walls. "The new baby is going to be a preemie."

I was trembling and had to tell myself to stop. Quick as I could, I switched on the lights, first in the hall and then in my room and in the bathroom. I couldn't bear to stay in the dark another minute.

I got into jeans and a t-shirt swiftly. I was frightened for all of us, but most of all for the tiny baby ten weeks too young. *Ten weeks!* I had been nine weeks too early. This baby was even younger.

Older folks like to say that history repeats itself. Well, if that's so, I'm alive and I'm fine. That eased my terror a bit.

Suddenly, I cared very much for the baby, boy or girl. Either one. The baby's sex didn't matter to my parents; even though there was a test my mother could have taken, she hadn't bothered. "I'd like it to be a surprise," she'd said.

What a good time we'd had looking forward to the baby's birth! My parents were so happy. I understood all that better now; boy or girl, either would be terrific.

Right down the hall from my room, there was a freshly painted nursery, soft white with purple molding, and in there stood my old crib, reassembled, and some of my baby toys: the ball clown that tinkled when it rolled, the rubber duck that squeaked, and, my favorite, the sea horse mobile that floated above the crib and shone magically in the dark.

We Andersens were all ready for this baby. Oh, if only this baby was ready for us!

Hurrying to my parents' bedroom, I knocked on the door, and my father let me in. Only the small nightlight was on. My mother, dressed in her navy blue jumper, was lying down, her eyes closed, her knees drawn up tight to her body. She was very pale. One arm lay on top of the flowered patchwork quilt.

I touched her fingers. They were cold. "Mom?"

"Yes, darling. Don't be frightened."

"The ambulance will be here in a few minutes," my father said. He stood at the window and peered through the Venetian blind watching for it.

"I rested," my mother said, softly, "and I've been so careful about proteins and vitamins and minerals. I drank only bottled water. I didn't touch so much as one teaspoonful of wine during the entire pregnancy. I watched everything. *Everything.*"

My father came alongside the bed and stroked my mother's face. "Nora, you did everything you could."

My mother would not be comforted. "Did I eat the wrong food? Did I overwork? Did I forget something?" A huge tear appeared at the inner corner of each of her eyes.

I got a tissue and wiped them away. "I love you, Mom," I whispered. "It's not your fault."

My mother managed a shaky smile. "Thanks, love. I guess I know that. I remember when you were born, the same silly old wives' tales—superstitions that I always laugh at—popped into my head."

Like stepping on the cracks, I thought.

She groaned then and scrunched up her face. Just then, the ambulance pulled into our driveway, and, in minutes, my mother was safely inside it and on her way.

Dad and I drove behind the ambulance. At that hour there was no traffic.

"Daddy, can I ask a question?"

"You sure can. But you also may."

"Why did this happen? Why did it happen twice to Mom?"

He was following the ambulance carefully. "No one knows, Asa. Medical people understand a tremendous amount, but often not the reason a baby isn't carried to term. About half of all premature births are from unknown causes."

I just sat silently after that, through our arrival and the first strange hours in the hospital, a great confusion of sirens and lights and beepers and bells, and the loudspeaker paging doctors.

Children were not allowed inside, so I ended up in the brightly lit waiting area. My father kept disappearing and then coming back. "No news," he'd say each time. "No news is good news." He'd sit for a few minutes and then go off again.

One other person was waiting. A bald plump man with a thick black mustache. His name was Mahoney and his wife was having twins. After a while, a nurse came to tell Mr. Mahoney he had two new daughters, each weighing a bit more than five pounds.

He handed me one fat cigar then a second one. "They're for your dad," he said. "Good luck to all of you."

He was so happy, I didn't tell him my father didn't smoke.

"Good luck to you, too, and to the new babies." I couldn't resist asking, "Do you have names for them yet?"

"Demi and Uma," he said proudly. "My wife's favorite actresses. It don't matter who gets which. The babies are identical."

I watched him hurrying away to have a look at his twins. The names were very peculiar. Poor babies. It was hard enough to be identical. How could an identical twin be *herself*? And how could she be herself with a famous person's name?

When you said the name Demi or the name Uma, a face came along connected to each name. Suppose these Mahoney babies grew up not pretty or talented and they had those names?

Well, the thirteen Ingrids didn't look anything like

the great actress, and, somehow, they survived. So it was possible. But people seemed to be giving sillier names every year.

When *I* have children, I promised myself, I will name them something like Mary and John. Nice plain names. Inconspicuous names.

A crew of new nurses and doctors came on duty and the tired ones went home. It was bright morning by the time my father came back to the waiting room.

I saw him coming and ran toward him. "Mr. Mahoney had daughters: Demi and Uma. He left you these cigars."

"Demi and Uma? Really?" He was amused. "And we have a boy—Leif Beowulf Andersen."

A boy! Leif was the name they'd favored all along. It was for Leif Ericson who had discovered Vineland. But the middle name? "Did you say Bearwolf, Daddy?"

"No. Beowulf. He's named after the great Norse hero who killed the dragon, Grendel."

Demi, Uma, and Leif Beowulf in one morning? Maybe there was something in the air in this hospital. My father shut his eyes and for a moment just stood there rubbing his lids gently with the backs of his hands. I had never seen him so tired.

Looking at him I suddenly knew I loved him very much, him and my mother, even if they were weird on the subject of names. Who knows, the name Beowulf might be lucky for the baby and help him to be strong. A dragon-killer is not your ordinary, everyday preemie. Anyway, boys didn't care so much about their names. And if he hated it, he could keep it secret the way I kept Alfifa secret. I would help him.

"Are they both okay? Daddy, tell me what happened!"

My father pulled his opened shirt collar loose so it was far away from his neck and slumped against the wall. "They're okay, Asa, but they've had a long tough time. The baby is tiny. And fragile. He weighs a little more than two pounds." He sighed softly.

"There was a bad minute in there. The baby didn't make a sound after he was born. The room was so silent that Mom and I were terrified. She couldn't bear it, and she screamed, 'Cry, Leif baby, cry. Oh, please, please, cry!'"

Now my father looked immensely pleased. "It was as if he understood her, and he gave a weak little cry, a peep, like a small, frightened chick. It was the most beautiful sound we'd ever heard. I wish I'd had a tape recorder. It was the sound of life. A beautiful new life!"

Poor Leif. When he grew up, they would tell this story about him. That he was such a genius, he heard his mother telling him to cry right after he was born, and he understood and obeyed.

They would know it was utterly impossible, but they'd tell it anyway and secretly believe it. Even my father, the principal, would believe it in his heart. Parents are pretty odd.

"They're putting him in an incubator in the Neonatal Intensive Care Unit. That's the special room for premature babies."

"Is that where I—"

"Yes. You started out in the same ICU." He gave me a wicked look. "Maybe that's why you used to love that game: 'Peekaboo! I C U!'"

"Daddy!"

He smiled at me. "Look how terrific you are today."

"How's Mom?"

"She's very tired, but she'll be fine. You'll get to see her later on. I don't know when you'll see Leif. We'll have to find out what the rules are—and if they make exceptions. Come, Asa, it's certainly time to go home."

"No school today, Daddy?"

"Not for you. I'll go to work, but you're going home to sleep."

"Yippee! I get to play hookey at last!"

"You can thank your kid brother for that."

I grinned. I had quite a kid brother. Though he wasn't very big yet, this day off was a good sign. He weighed less than three pounds, yet he was already doing me favors. When he grew up, I might mention to him how right after he was born . . .

Uh uh. I stopped myself. I'm doing it, too. Creating a family legend and I'm not even a parent. I'll never mention it to him. But I will train him early to keep doing me favors.

I'll help him see how lucky he is to have an older sister who faced down a Tarheel in a bitter name war. He'll need me, and I'll be right there.

To train him early and to train him well.

That was the key to being a successful big sister.

9

Peekaboo! ICU!

I dragged myself up the stairs and fell into bed in my clothes. I had never been this beat.

When daytime came it didn't matter that I had been too tired to close the blinds and the room filled with light—I slept.

If a brass band had come marching through playing "When the Saints Come Marching In" full blast, I wouldn't have stirred.

When I did wake, I made a major decision: *I would make dinner for my father and myself!* The pudgeball was no more; this was the decision of a confident sylph.

Major, because I didn't know beans about cooking. (I didn't even know how to cook beans.) Since my mother always enjoyed preparing the meals, I'd never bothered to do anything but eat.

But I could read directions on boxes. And the kitchen cabinets were chock-full of food. My mother always had enough supplies on hand in case of famine or drought.

It took me way over an hour to prepare the dinner. One pound of spaghetti turned out to be much-too-much. It was now sagging snugly in the colander. There was tomato sauce with mushrooms, and a terrific salad: lettuce, tomatoes, cucumbers, carrots, watercress, olives, and croutons sprinkled on top. Then I found a jar of artichoke hearts and added those.

"Beautiful salad," my father said. "Plenty of *lettuce*—appropriate in honor of *Leif*."

I was pleased. "Sorry about the soft spaghetti," I said. "I just didn't want it to be raw."

"No problem," my father said. "I like it mushy. Why do you think they call it pasta? It means paste—all it is is flour and water. I think you did a great job, Asa. Wait till Mom hears."

He kissed me on the forehead. "Tonight I'm going to take Leif's picture with my Polaroid, so you can see him."

I couldn't wait. While clearing up and washing the dishes, I hoped and prayed harder than I ever had before.

My mother and Leif had to come home well, and

I would cook an incredible spaghetti dinner—not mushy—for all of them.

Well, Leif could, at least, smell the sauce.

Just so they came home safe. My father was coming back with pictures, and I would actually be able to see *him!*

I sat myself down right near the door, waiting. I must have nodded off to sleep in the chair because hours later the car drove into the garage. In a minute my father was standing there in the doorway with a handful of pictures.

I took them eagerly and settled down to study them. They were remarkably clear—and in them the baby was small, so incredibly small, the nurse held him wholly cradled in the palm of one hand.

He was bald and scrawny like some marvelous stone carving.

My new brother! That seemed a most remarkable thing. He certainly is not beautiful. Some people might even find him ugly, but they better not say so when I'm around. He's so tiny, he really will need someone to fight his battles for him. That'll be my job.

He doesn't have eyelashes or eyebrows or hair. Yet, he is somehow very beautiful, he is wonderful, he is the most beautiful baby ever born. There is no one else in the world like him. I will never forget how he looks here.

I held the pictures up under the light and squinched up my eyes so I could study them closely. "Is there anything wrong with him, Daddy?" I asked finally.

"Nothing. He's perfect. He's just too young. Born too soon. He didn't have enough time to grow and develop so he could live independently."

Again, I went over the pictures as carefully as I could. "Did I look like that?"

"The spitting image. Especially the spitting part."

Why do parents remember *everything?*

"I'm glad I grew hair." I looked at the baby again. So small, so impossibly small. To be the parent of an infant that tiny was probably the scariest thing that could happen to a grown-up.

Some things began to be clear to me that I had never really understood before. No wonder my mother had babied me for so long, had stuffed me like a turkey all those years, wanting me to be large. When such a tiny baby is born, the mother *must* believe that big means beautiful, that huge equals healthy.

Who could ever have imagined being that tiny size?

Dr. Hamburger had understood my mother perfectly, but I had been miles from understanding what was happening until this very moment.

Fear and love and the need to protect the small helpless creature taken from her to the incubator and kept there for months—those were the reasons for the years of breakfast trays.

My mother, locked into memories of me as small and completely helpless, had been unable to see me grow. Even though I was growing right there before her eyes! Growing? I ballooned.

When Leif got bigger, if my mother brought out the breakfast tray and started overstuffing him, I swore to myself that I would remind her, stop her, help him. To help them both.

For the next few days, I moved about in a kind of waking-sleep. People were very kind at school. Miss Kahn had told the class that I had a new, very small baby brother in the ICU.

Even the Tarheel had the decency to leave me alone.

Felicia gave me a lovely blue rattle shaped like a dolphin for Leif. It tinkled whenever it was touched. "My grandmother sent it," Felicia said. "And I want you to tell your mother I'd be glad to help baby-sit. For free."

"Thanks," I said, "but that's my job."

"Let me help, too, Asa. Friends have to share."

"Sure," I agreed. "You can change his diapers."

Felicia shrugged. "Poop doesn't bother me."

"Really?"

"I just don't pay it any mind."

My mother, pale and thin, but well, came home. Leif did not. He had to stay.

Then began the shuttle; my parents were constantly going back and forth to the hospital. I spent a lot of time alone.

Felicia invited me over, but I didn't feel like it. I felt like staying alone so I could wish, wish, wish! I needed to concentrate on wishing.

One afternoon, I accompanied my mother to the hospital and was sitting in the waiting room when the Head Nurse of the Neonatal Intensive Care Unit came for me.

"Would you like to come and have a look at your brother?" she asked.

Like all the nurses, she wore a plastic name badge. Hers said "Glinda." She took off her glasses, which then hung from a chain about her neck, and smiled. "Want to come?"

She had the kindest, sweetest, gentlest face I'd ever seen. Her bright yellow hair seemed like spun gold. Her name was no accident: Glinda was the Good Witch of the North. The long metal pin darting through her hair was no knitting-needle. It was surely a wand.

I nearly knocked her over flying out of my chair.

"I guess you *would* like to see him. Your mother

thought so. Come along. We'll have to put you in scrubs."

"Scrubs?"

"Green uniforms. They're special sanitary clothes we wear in the operating room and the ICU."

I put on the rough, green, loose shirt and pants and felt like a stalk of broccoli. Oh, how I wished Felicia could see me. But only Felicia.

This was a one-size-fits-nobody outfit. Then I pulled on a puffy plastic shower cap and went in to a wonderful baby-saving room right out of science fiction.

Imagine a vast, brightly lit white ward filled with incubators wired to all sorts of monitors; bells and beepers going off constantly, and all the staff dressed like jolly green elves.

There was continual activity all around: stalks of broccoli on the alert, charging about, conferring. A sweet female voice repeatedly paged various specialists, doctors and nurses suddenly dashed to huddle around an incubator, sometimes drawing the curtain while they did mysterious things.

It sounded a lot like a video game gallery—with the lights and the whirring and pinging noises from the monitors—only here they were playing for the biggest prize of all: life.

My mother and father stood on either side of the

small white compartment covered by clear plastic. The incubator was just a little bigger than a refrigerator tray.

I looked in and got my first glimpse of my brother, that tiny tiny baby with tubes going into him—one into his neck and one into his belly button—and all sorts of wires from machines attached to him.

He had soft, almost transparent skin through which ran tiny veins like blue threads. His legs were so thin they could have belonged to a bird.

And, yes, my father was right, when he cried the sound was more like a baby chick's than a human's.

He was wearing a cute, blue stocking cap.

"Is he cold?" I wondered.

My mother, who was smiling down at the baby, nodded. "He isn't able to maintain normal body temperature, so the incubator keeps him warm. And they bundle him up."

"What're the tubes for?"

"The one in his throat—his trachea—helps him breathe. The one to his stomach feeds him."

"And those wires, Mom?"

"They're monitoring his heart and his breathing rate and his blood pressure and the amount of oxygen in his blood."

"It's scary," I said.

My mother put her arm around me and hugged me.

"Yes, it is. Are you sorry you came in here, Asa? You don't have to stay if it frightens you."

"Oh, no. I'm old enough. I'm his older sister. I'm going to take care of him."

Suddenly the loudspeaker began calling, "Code—One East. Emergency!" over and over, and the doctors and nurses quickly headed toward one little baby on the other side of the room where two nurses were already working.

Immediately, one of the nurses pulled the curtain so its white folds enclosed the crowd around the incubator.

When the curtain was finally opened, after a very long time, the doctors and nurses came walking away briskly, some talking and smiling, and most of them looking relieved.

"Everything's fine," Glinda the Good said as she went past us silent Andersens. "That baby is now sound asleep. The little ones do keep us running."

"The most terrible thing," my mother said, "is to be in another part of the hospital and hear that message, 'Code—One East. Emergency!' You know it's the Neonatal Intensive Care Unit and you think it might be your baby."

We stood around watching Leif sleep. When he moved slightly, my mother and father took turns talking to him, and they encouraged me to talk to him, too. "He'll hear your voice, and he'll get to know it," my father said. "Babies are really very smart, and they learn lots of things. The sooner you start teaching them the better.

"Mom and I will go to the coffee bar and get some coffee while you keep Leif company. You can talk to him or sing to him. Anything you like. Okay?"

"I'd love it," I said. "I'm baby-sitting my kid brother. First time, so I'll do it free, but then we'll have to talk about my rates."

My parents laughed and went off leaving me standing there next to Leif, and I told him softly how much I loved him and that I was looking forward to him coming home.

Next, I sang several *Sesame Street* songs, and then, to my own surprise, began to tell him the story of the three bears.

Of course, he couldn't possibly understand it, but I liked telling it and changing my voice. Especially into Papa Bear. After a while, I ducked my head to one side and tried, "Peekaboo. I see you," but there wasn't much point to that since his eyes were tightly shut. He couldn't have seen me anyway, even if his eyes were open, because—my mother had said—newborns don't see too well at first.

I noticed that some of the incubators were decorated with drawings and stuffed toys and photographs, and I decided that next time I came I would bring a small family picture and the tiny, soft, black-and-white felt penguin I'd bought.

Once or twice the baby moved quickly—his movements were so jerky, they frightened me—but then he settled down. I was very glad to see my mother and father come back.

Finally, my parents said good-bye to Lief, who, of course didn't take the slightest notice.

"*Hasta mañana*," I told him. My parents looked surprised, so I quoted my father right back to himself. "The sooner you start teaching him the better."

"But how—" my father began.

"Felicia's grandmother. You know I call for Felicia every morning? Well, Mrs. Rodriguez answers the door and she doesn't speak a word of English. If I want to say anything to her, I have to do it in Spanish."

I felt proud of myself. My parents really admired learning—learning *anything*. They were beaming now, as I explained.

"So, I'm learning. I call it 'Grandma Spanish.' I'm pretty good with *muy bien* and *sí* and stuff like that.

"And I'm glad to pass it along to the *bebé*, to Lief."

10

Code One East— Emergency

Back in school, things went along peacefully. Robert Edward Lee left me alone, perhaps because I spent a lot of time sending him silent brain wave messages:

> *You'd better keep out of my face because if you start with me again, I'll destroy you.*
> *I have too many important things on my mind to waste time with a Tarheel bully.*
> *Next time, I'll drown your precious album.*

He could tell from my straight back and my no-nonsense attitude that I meant business. When I had to pass papers or books back to him, I flipped them over my shoulder without turning around. I never once looked directly at him. He had to know that as far as I was concerned, he did not exist. Period.

"Asa," Miss Kahn asked me privately, "do you want to talk to the class about your brother and what it's like in the hospital?"

She was gentle. "Your classmates are concerned and I am, too. We are sort of a second family here. What happens to you affects all of us. And the information — about the ICU — would be very interesting to many." She paused. "But if you'd rather keep it private, that's entirely up to you. Think about it."

Later, I asked Felicia, "Should I?"

"I think so. Mei, Anita, even that flake Sandra, and a lot of the other kids keep asking me how you're doing and if your brother's okay. You know, your father being principal makes everyone notice something is going on. And guess who else asked — Ramon."

"Ramon talked to you? Why didn't you tell me?"

"I *am* telling you. Now."

"Did he stutter? Did he speak English or Spanish?"

"English. And, boy, did he stutter. So, I said speak Spanish so the others won't understand, and," Felicia smiled, "he did — and he didn't stutter once. But he'd rather talk in English."

"What did he want to know?"

"Oh, just how your kid brother was doing. How little he was. Did you actually get to see him? Things like that."

"I'm so glad he spoke to you, Felicia."

"Me, too. I—I have a feeling he was asking about your brother for himself—and for someone else, too."

"Who?" I saw whom she meant by the expression on her face. "You're crazy."

Felicia shook her head hard. "He said he was asking because 'people wanted to know.' What 'people' does he hang out with? The two Tarheels. And I'm sure it wasn't Tommy Lee who wanted to know."

I had a lot of trouble with that. The snake that sat behind me had a heart? Hard to believe.

"Well, that is hot news. You know, this baby Leif isn't even normal size and he's changing the world already," I marveled.

"Yeah," Felicia said. "When you name a kid for a dragon-killer, you better watch out! Next time you see Bearwolf tell him to keep up the good work."

"Not Bearwolf. Beowulf."

Felicia was stubborn. "He'll always be Bearwolf to me. I like it better."

Uh, uh, it's beginning, I thought. Give a child a peculiar name and he's in for it. But Leif has me to help him. And I will! Don't worry, little brother. I'm here. Sticks and stones . . .

"By the way, Asa, what happened to alliteration? Your folks didn't give the baby names with repeat sounds like yours."

"I don't know. Maybe they took the hint from me

that it's not the best way to start someone off in life. Leif is lucky."

Felicia's eyebrows rose. *"Leif Bearwolf?"*

"You're right."

I decided to talk to the class about Leif. If they wanted to know, if even the most heartless among them was interested, then the information might as well come directly from me. Otherwise, there might be all kinds of stories.

So, in the afternoon, during the ten-minute period set aside for class meeting, I sat at my desk and told them about the doctors and nurses in broccoli-colored scrubs, and the ICU with all its machines and beepers and bells and lights.

I told them about the tiny tiny babies smaller than most dolls, lying in the little plastic-covered bins decorated with pictures and toys, their families hanging around, hoping.

"Let us send your little brother a happy birthday card," Anita suggested, "to welcome him."

"Come on. It would have to be a first-birthday-minus-one card," Tommy Lee argued. "He won't be one for a whole year."

"Right," his cousin, of course, agreed with him. "You can't send a minus-one birthday card."

Mei, sitting way up front, half-stood in her seat and waved her hand frantically.

When Miss Kahn called on her, she said, "In China, a baby's first birthday is the day he is born. So let us send a Chinese card. I can bring a beautiful one tomorrow."

Even the Tarheels agreed this was a fine solution. I promised to tape the class card to the incubator. Class meeting ended and we turned to social studies.

It was a review winding up the unit on the Civil War.

With all the time I'd been spending at the hospital, I was completely out of it. I had not done any of the reading yet.

So, I listened as Miss Kahn summarized the previous lessons: The old plantation system made it possible for the south to grow cotton cheaply, but that system depended on slavery. "Is owning another person and making him work for you a good thing?" she asked.

"No!" My classmates were unanimous.

"Is there anyone in here who would like to own a slave?"

"Just to do my homework," Tommy Lee called out for a laugh.

"Tommy!" Miss Kahn reproved him. "Is there anyone here who would want to be a slave?"

The room was still.

Miss Kahn reminded us that the southern states, angry that the northern states were restricting slavery in many ways, seceded from the Union and formed the

Confederacy. That broke up the country and the two sides went to war.

"Why was it called the 'Civil' War?" Anita asked. "I believe the word civil means polite, respectful."

Tommy Lee hooted. "It sure wasn't a polite war."

Miss Kahn quieted Tommy with a teacher-look. "Good question. You all know that a word can have several meanings. Civil does mean polite and respectful. It comes from the Latin word for citizen. This was a war among citizens, a long, bloody war which sometimes split families—brother fought brother."

Miss Kahn further noted that early on in the war, President Lincoln emancipated the slaves.

"Emancipated means what? Ramon?"

"Freed," Ramon said, so fast he forgot to stutter. Even he was surprised.

"Good!" Miss Kahn smiled.

"I am named for the greatest general of the whole Civil War," came the voice from behind me, suddenly. "General Robert E. Lee."

"What can you tell us about him?" Miss Kahn asked.

"He was a Southerner, born in Virginia. He didn't believe in secession or slavery—and he loved the Union—but he was loyal to Virginia. So he led Virginia's troops, and he later became the greatest Confederate General."

I hated all this boasting, but since I hadn't done the reading, I couldn't argue with him.

Felicia, however, understood exactly what friends were for. Her hand shot up. "He lost," she said.

Felicia, who loved social studies, *had* read the assignment carefully, especially the parts about General Robert Edward Lee. She was so surprised to find the name in her book, she had tried to call me up, but I was over at the hospital.

"Lee lost at Gettysburg, and the war ended when he surrendered his sword at Appo — Appo — "

"Appomattox," the Tarheel finished for her. "Sure he lost. He didn't have enough trained soldiers or supplies. But everyone knows how brave and smart he was. He was one of the bravest and smartest strategists of his time."

"But he still lost," Felicia reminded him again.

I could hear angry moving in the seat behind me.

"Lee did lose," Miss Kahn said, "but many historians do consider him the greatest general of the Civil War. Robert, you have an illustrious name."

Tommy reached way over to give his cousin a high five.

He had to do that, I thought. He had to get the message out that *his* name wasn't soggy, drippy dregs. He had to show off. That means I really got to him. Serves him right, the bully.

There was a loud rapping at our classroom door and then it flew open before Miss Kahn could get to it.

My father came through the doorway of Room 404.

"Excuse me," he said to the class, and then he spoke softly but urgently to Miss Kahn for a moment.

"Asa," she said, "please come to the desk."

My heart plummeted.

"Get your coat, honey," my father said quietly. "Come to my office, and be quick. We've got to get over to the hospital."

I knew from the pain in his eyes. CODE ONE EAST—EMERGENCY. And this time it was Leif.

My own eyes brimming with tears, I dumped everything into my bookbag. Felicia brought my coat.

"The baby?" she whispered.

I was afraid to answer because I knew I was about to cry. My lips were trembling and my chin wobbling. I nodded.

Felicia squeezed my arm and went back to her seat.

My father piloted the car at a speed he'd never reached before. We were nearly there before he spoke, and then it was in answer to my silent question. "Mom is there waiting for us."

I was numb. There was so much I wanted to ask, so much I wanted to say to my father, but couldn't.

He drove into the hospital parking lot and when he'd switched off the ignition, he turned to me and said gently, "The baby is having trouble breathing, Asa. We have to be strong for Mom, and help each other."

On the hospital steps stood my mother, her hand shading her eyes, looking out for us. Her face was weary and pale and her silky blonde hair blew loose and straggly in the spring wind.

She looked so terribly tired. She had obviously rushed from the house the minute they called her.

She kissed us both. "No change," she said sadly.

Then she hugged me close. "The baby is not getting enough oxygen," she explained. "It's called Respiratory Distress Syndrome. It happened to you, too, soon after you were born," my mother tried to smile, but it didn't quite work, "and look at you now. You're fine."

Then she began to weep, and we stood close and comforted her. After several minutes, she lifted her head and took a deep breath. "I'm all right now." She went into the Ladies Room and came out washed and neatly combed. "Forgive me," she said. "I felt so alone before you got here. I needed my family with me."

Once we were inside, my mother kept her arm around my shoulders tightly. At times, I could hardly breathe, but I knew I was helping just by being there.

We waited, in a corner of the waiting area under the white lights, a small huddle of silent, frightened people, a family with a loved one in danger—three helpless human beings.

All we could do was wait, and hope, and pray. And that's what we did.

In my mind's eye I saw inside the ICU: a white curtain was drawn all around a bin holding a very very little boy with a big name. Doctors and nurses dressed in scruffy green were watching him and doing things with wires and needles and oxygen.

Save him, I begged silently, *Save him, save him. Save my little brother!*

Kind members of the staff came by urging us to sit down, to go get Cokes or coffee, to take a walk, but we didn't budge. Somehow it seemed better not to change anything, not to move, till the danger was past. It was a time of such terror that the slightest wrong move might tip the universe. We stayed fixed in place.

Then Nurse Glinda came and took my mother's hand. "He's sleeping peacefully," she said, "and he's fine. He gave us a scare, but he's absolutely okay."

First, we sat down on the bench close to one another, and we rested in silence for a while. A long while.

I spent the time saying thank you, thank you, thank you in my head. I said four hundred thanks yous before I stopped.

My father stirred first. "You know what I feel like doing?" he said. "I feel like taking my two favorite women out to dinner. To celebrate."

"Don't you think we should just go home so we're near the phone, Martin?" My mother smiled nervously.

"No. I'll call the hospital from the restaurant and give them the number. We can get back here in minutes. The restaurant I have in mind is right nearby, closer than our own house."

My mother agreed, "But let's stop back in here on our way home."

"Sure thing." My father was delighted.

We rarely ate out. Why go to restaurants when you've got a superb live-in cook? But this was a kind of birthday celebration—even if the guest of honor was back in the hospital being fed by tube.

The small restaurant was French. *CHEZ SUZETTE* was its name and Suzette herself welcomed us.

She was red-haired, a very glamorous older woman in a slinky black dress slit to her thigh with black lace stockings peeping out. Black velvet pumps with rhinestone buckles completed her outfit. The buckles matched her glittery dangling earrings. She smelled like a flower garden.

I'd seen such outfits on TV and in the movies, but

Suzette was the first actual woman I met dressed that way. Her dress clung like plastic wrap.

I decided to get an outfit just like Suzette's when I was grown. Slit dress, lace stockings, black velvet pumps with rhinestone buckles; the works! Then I would be as beautiful as Ingrid. Perhaps more beautiful.

It was a tiny restaurant; all together there were only eight tables. We were the first customers of the evening. There were white linen tablecloths, and linen napkins the size of diapers, and on each table was a crystal vase of lovely cream-colored roses.

"If this is your first visit here, perhaps you will permit me to recommend the specials," Suzette suggested in a heavy French accent. "And the lovely young lady must have a menu of her own to choose from and to keep." She handed me one, but it was all in French!

My parents chattered away with her in French for a few minutes and then my father said, "*Bon.* We are in your hands."

Well, my parents may have put us in Suzette's hands, but when the first dish came—snails—I climbed out of her hands.

"Snails! *Escargot à la bourguignonne?*" Suzette offered.

"No, thank you," I said. Snails, yuck! but I had the good sense not to say it.

My parents enjoyed the strange dish. I, meanwhile, chewed slowly on a single slice of crusty French bread, doing my best not to watch what was going on. The snails themselves didn't look bad. It was the *idea* of eating them that was upsetting.

Then we all had onion soup, which came in earthenware casseroles topped with thick melted cheese.

Suzette went into the kitchen and brought out her husband, Henri, a handsome man with dark, curly hair and a mustache, wearing a huge chef's hat, who suggested the special, duck *á l'orange*.

My dad decided enthusiastically. "Trust me, Asa. This duck dish, well-prepared, is out of this world!" While we were waiting, my father began gravely. "You know the French are a people of great culture . . ."

Uh oh, I thought. A lecture!

"Because they are so cultured," he continued, "it is difficult to believe that they go about *oui oui-ing* everywhere."

"Oh, Martin," my mother laughed. "You're hopeless."

I blushed. "I didn't think principals told jokes like that, Daddy."

"Principals, my girl, are like everybody else."

"Only worse," my mother added.

A platter of duck came, and it was out of this world: soft, juicy chunks of duck covered with crisp skin that was soaked in orange sauce. With it came *haricots verts*, which turned out to be green beans, and *pommes frites*, real French fries.

Twice, while we were eating, the phone up front rang.

Twice, we stopped eating and breathing while Suzette hurried to answer it.

Both times, she waved away our fears with a big gesture and spoke loudly to her caller in French. I would learn French after I finished learning Spanish. I would be a great linguist and understand everyone.

I finished everything on my plate. Then came the great test. Seconds. I refused. And, when Henri wheeled over a little cart full of incredible chocolate and cream pastries and cheeses, I had to force my mouth to say, "No, thank you. I don't care for any." (It was a lie! I cared.)

My mother and father chose some really foul-smelling cheeses along with biscuits. My eyes stayed glued on the éclairs.

My mom noticed and she had a pre-Doctor Hamburger relapse. "Can we get an éclair for our daughter to take out?" she asked, and, in seconds, Henri had packed one in a white cardboard box.

We headed back to the hospital. Nurse Glinda was still on duty. "Just in time," she said. "I'm about to go on my coffee break, but I'm delighted to tell you, Leif is fine. He's slept beautifully all the time you were away. I think he'll have a good night, so you should, too."

Joy filled me, and I knew just how to celebrate. "Please," I said to her, "may I give you a present?"

"Well, that's very thoughtful of you, but you needn't—"

I handed her the pastry box. "It's for your coffee break. Because I'm so happy."

"*CHEZ SUZETTE*," she read the label on the box. "How elegant."

"It's only an éclair."

"Only! Instead of Dunkin' Donuts?"

"It's from me and Leif."

"You mean Leif and me," my father corrected.

"Whatever. Like my dad is always on grammar duty," I complained to the nurse. She went off smiling.

"Did I hear that child just start a sentence with *like?*" my father demanded, as we walked through the deserted hospital lobby.

"*Oui, oui, oui,*" Mom said enthusiastically.

"We'd better get your mother home quickly, Asa," he said. "She's starting to *oui oui* all over the place."

They were being silly. How I loved it!

11

The Bambino

I opened one eye, squinted at my clock and saw 11:09. I was all confused, not sure where I was, or what day it was.

Then the first-awakening fog began to clear. Slowly, some joyous sensations came to me: I was lying in my own soft, warm bed; it was the morning following Leif's CODE ONE EAST-EMERGENCY and it was a school day.

My mother must have let me oversleep.

"Thank you, baby brother," I whispered into my quilt, and then I yelled, as if I were really upset, "Mom. Mom! Why didn't you wake me up for school?"

"You were exhausted." My mother came in and started to open the blinds. "I thought to myself, Asa can miss this day of school. We'll just take it easy this morning, and then we'll go over and visit the baby this afternoon. Daddy will join us there."

"Is he still sleeping?"

That gave her a laugh. "*You* can miss a day of school but he can't. He insisted on going. By the way, Felicia's grandmother phoned early this morning to find out—"

"Felicia's grandmother? What are you talking about? She doesn't speak English. Not even two or three words."

"I know you told us that, Asa dear, but Mrs. Rodriguez phoned me about eight-thirty this morning, when you didn't come to pick Felicia up. She was worried. She knew about the emergency yesterday and wanted to find out if the baby was all right."

I lay back on my pillow and considered this wacky story. "I don't know who you talked to on the phone, Mom, but it couldn't have been Mrs. Rodriguez. It couldn't have been, Mom! Felicia has to translate everything for her. Maybe it was Felicia."

"Asa, wouldn't I know Felicia's voice? She's called here hundreds of times."

"Then it's a mystery."

"She said it was Mrs. Rodriguez calling."

"Impossible."

My mother dropped the subject.

I wondered about it as I lazied around, took a long

shower, and wrapped the big, black bath towel around my body so it had a slit like Suzette's dress and a leg and thigh peeked out.

My legs seemed nice. I imagined them in dark lacy stockings. Velvet pumps with rhinestone buckles. Mmmm. I'd be a knockout one day. That was my plan. If anyone came along and said—What is your ambition, Asa Andersen?—I would have to answer truthfully: To be a knockout in a slit skirt. Maybe a firefighter, or a great scientist who solves the problem of premature babies, but, best of all, a knockout.

My thoughts kept returning to the mysterious telephone call. Someone had played a trick on my mother.

Everyone in the grade knew Felicia and I were best friends. But what was the point of phoning? And pretending to be Mrs. Rodriguez?

Tomorrow morning I would get Felicia to tell her grandmother all about the phone call, and the old lady would be astonished. I could already imagine her face.

That was for tomorrow. Meanwhile, today was mine.

A day when every other kid is at school, but you are lucky enough to be at home, not sick but idling, is a prize. And if you happen to be the principal's daughter, it may come only once or twice in your lifetime, if at all. Nothing is quite like it.

I decided to polish my toenails. Sexy legs required

fiery Turbulent Red, but I had to settle for Dusty Pink, my mother's standard polish. I would buy my own bottle of red as soon as I could.

I experimented with different hairstyles. Loose was very glamorous, but not easy to control. I put a folded sock in each cup of the training bra just to see the future. It was effective, though the shape left something to be desired. Socks, even thick ones, are still only socks.

I watched TV. I listened to tapes. I got into jeans and a sky blue oxford button-down shirt, rolling up the sleeves and tucking in the tails, so I'd be ready when my mother was. The unexplained telephone call was a continual teaser no matter what I did. I was ready when my mother called me.

When we got to the hospital, the baby had just been bathed and weighed and dressed. He had a sweet smell—baby powder and lotions, probably.

The power of my feeling for Leif amazed me. Just looking at him was pleasure, was wonder, was not like any other experience I'd had. I loved him so much! How was this possible? I hardly knew him. I *didn't* know him. What was to know? He'd just been born.

Who, the question nagged me, had taken the occasion of his birth to tease my mother on the telephone?

It wasn't a male voice so I couldn't blame the Tarheel. Since it wasn't a dirty phone call or a mean phone call, it made no sense. It was pointless.

Leif had gained three ounces! My mother was allowed to hold him and feed him. Apparently, he was mighty hungry because he chomped away on that nipple as if it were a steak, his eyes tightly shut, his tiny cheeks pumping.

Next, I had a turn feeding him, but I was very nervous. So nervous, my arms shook with excitement. Holding him so his head rested safely on the crook of my arm, I tipped the bottle and watched him. He was so incredibly tiny. And cute. And unbelievable. What if I dropped him?

"Leif is making me tremble like a leaf. Please, Mom," I handed him back to my mother. "Sorry. I'm a little nervous."

"Of course you are," she said, "but you'll be amazed at how quickly you'll learn."

The baby paused in his feeding for an instant to smile, his eyes still tightly scrunched up. New babies are not supposed to be able to smile, but he did.

Then I changed my mind and longed to hold him again, but kept quiet about it. He was a baby, not a basketball to be passed back and forth. He was chewing away again making funny little sucking noises. Suction noises really. I bet the two words came from the same beginning. Probably.

"When do you think he can he come home?" I asked.

"Well, he has to weigh more. He's already eating by mouth, so if he keeps a normal temperature without the incubator, and he has regular breathing and heart rates, then he'll be ready."

"Are you scared to take care of him, Mom? I mean he'll still be so small."

"Not as scared as I was with you, Asa. You were so tiny and I was so inexperienced. I had no confidence. But the hospital has a wonderful system. Three days before they discharge a preemie, they put the mother, the father, and the baby in a private room.

"That was when I first took care of you, and there were always people around to answer questions. I could open the door and yell 'Help!' if I needed to."

"Did you?"

"No. But knowing I could was what counted. I didn't sleep at all the first two nights. I just sat up watching you. I was afraid that without all those tubes and monitors and machines some terrible thing would happen. Nothing did, so the third night I slept. Then, at last, we went home."

"This time you'll have me to help, too."

"Yes. I'm counting on you," my mother smiled. "You and Dad."

"And Felicia. She loves babies. She doesn't even mind changing diapers."

"That's the real test of friendship." My mother was impressed. "I'll certainly have plenty of help."

A little after three, my father came bursting in. "I have a surprise for you," he told me, "in the waiting room."

The surprise was Felicia!

Remarkably, she and I were wearing identical outfits: pale blue oxford shirts with rolled sleeves, jeans, white Nikes. We both even had on navy socks.

"We don't have to telephone each other," Felicia said, hugging me. "We read each other's minds."

I immediately went to the question that had bothered me all day. "Felicia, somebody who said she was your grandmother called my mother this morning."

Felicia looked startled. "Who did?"

"Some woman, who spoke English, called and said she was Mrs. Rodriguez and wanted to know if the baby was okay."

"I don't know anything about that," Felicia said, uneasily. "You'll have to talk to my grandmother."

"But your grandmother—"

"I can't tell you anything about it, Asa." Felicia

looked very uncomfortable. "Tomorrow you can ask *Abuelita.*"

I stared at her. We were best friends, and I knew Felicia wasn't telling me something.

"Felicia—"

"I can't tell you anything about it, Asa. Don't ask me. Please." She began to rummage in her bookbag. "I came to bring the class greeting card to Leif." Carefully, she took a wide, cream-colored envelope out.

I opened it eagerly. There was a delicate black-and-white inked drawing of a baby asleep, a beautiful drawing. The printing was all in Chinese.

Since Felicia wasn't allowed into the Nursery, I kept her company outside until my parents had finished their visit. Then I gave them the card.

"Mei bought it for the class." I explained to my parents all about the birthday minus-one discussion and how this was absolutely the right card, the only possible card.

Names were written all over it in every blank space. Every student in the class—*everyone*—had signed and, of course, Miss Kahn, too.

"I brought Scotch tape," Felicia said, handing the spool over to my mom, "so you can stick the card on the incubator."

"We'll go back in and do that right now," Mom said.

"You must tell Miss Kahn and the class, and especially Mei, that it's a beautiful card and we'll keep it always."

After they'd disappeared inside, Felicia said, "I brought something else. You'll never guess what."

"I give up."

"You'll never guess who sent it, either."

"I gave up already."

"You have to at least try, Asa. Guess."

I studied my friend's face. She looked positively wicked.

"I'll give you a clue. It's a prize baseball card."

"No," I said, astounded. "It couldn't be him."

Felicia nodded. "Him who?"

"The Tarheel."

"Asa, you're a genius."

I sank down on the waiting room bench. "You're kidding."

"He gave it to Ramon to give to me to take to you."

"Why? How come?"

Felicia shrugged. "He said this is his prize card. It's Babe Ruth, the greatest baseball player of all time. His nickname was The Bambino—The Baby.

"He said it belongs on your brother's incubator. It'll bring good luck."

"Wait a minute. He said all that to Ramon, and Ramon said all that to you?"

"Yup. In English. And he only stuttered a very little."

"Let's see the card."

We looked at it together. It was in a small, plastic sleeve. Babe Ruth. "The Slugger." A funny-looking big guy with skinny legs clutching a bat, ready to swing.

"I hope Leif grows up better looking than that," I said, sourly, but I didn't feel sour at all.

I'd been wrong. The Tarheel had a heart, after all.

"Can you figure this, Felicia? I mean, can you?"

"I think he really likes you," Felicia said. "He likes you and he's sorry he was so mean."

I looked down at the card. "He must be *very* sorry. He nearly had a fit when he thought I wet this card."

"Go in and give it to your folks," Felicia said. "I promised I would get you to tape it on real tight so no one would steal it."

"Wait here. I'll be right back."

I went into the ICU. My father was holding Leif, cradling him and humming. I recognized the song: "As Time Goes By."

I looked fearfully to see if my mother was playing air piano where strangers might see her, but, luckily she was busy taping the birthday card to the side of the incubator.

"Mom, Dad, I've got something else for Leif." I held up the baseball card.

"A Babe Ruth card in mint condition!" My father was impressed. "Where'd you get that?"

"Felicia brought it. It came from someone in the class."

"That's a precious card to a collector, Asa." He frowned. "I don't know if we want to leave it here. It could get lost, or taken."

"Felicia said the kid who sent it wants Leif to have it near him. Because Babe Ruth was the great Bambino."

"Who sent it?" my mother asked.

"A boy in the class." I blushed. "He wants us to tape it on to the incubator—for luck."

"Give it here," my mother said. "Be sure to thank him, Asa. It's a wonderful gift."

We drove Felicia home. On the way I whispered in her ear, "What am I going to say to him tomorrow? I don't think I can even face him."

"Just say thank you. Don't make a big thing out of it."

"I don't know—it is a big thing. It's the biggest thing that ever happened to me in my whole life."

"Asa Alfifa Andersen, don't be dopey. This is his way of apologizing. All you have to do now is be nice."

We were in front of the Rodriguez house. "Be sure to wear something really special tomorrow," Felicia said quickly, as she gathered her stuff and started to get out of the car. "We can talk on the phone later and decide what."

"Thanks for the ride, Mr. Andersen, Mrs. Andersen."

"Please thank your grandmother for her kind call this morning," Mom said. "It was very thoughtful of her."

To my amazement, Felicia didn't say a word. She just sort of ducked her head.

"See you tomorrow morning, Asa. Come by early so you can talk to my grandmother. Bye." She ran up the stairs.

"She's a lovely girl." Mom watched till the door was shut with Felicia safely inside. "You're very lucky to have such a wonderful friend—to have such wonderful friends I should say—because the boy who sent the baseball card must be extraordinary."

"He is," I murmured, sinking down on the car seat and shutting my eyes so I could daydream.

Extraordinary. An extra-terrestrial.

12

Tomorrow

"**W**hat shall I wear to school tomorrow?" was the hot question of the evening.

As I ate my shrimp salad and the shrubbery that went with it (I was actually learning to like the stuff), I had an idea. So I sent up a trial balloon proposing a shopping trip to The Gap, only twenty minutes away.

My mother, with cool parental logic, quickly shot it down.

"First of all, you've got plenty of clothes," she said. "And, second of all, Daddy and I are exhausted. What we want to do most is sit in the living room and read till bedtime."

So I went and called Felicia, but she continued to be mysterious. More than mysterious. Secretive. Impossible.

Not one clue could be pried out of her, though I was positive she knew more than she would admit about the unexplained phone call.

"I thought you were my best friend," I said, "but you're hiding something from me."

"I *am* your best friend. I can't tell you anything."

"Some best friend—" I hung up on her abruptly.

Two minutes later, I panicked. Life would be unlivable without Felicia. Felicia must be behaving this way for a reason.

How could I have slammed down the phone on her? What reason?

I hardened my heart. Whatever reason, Felicia would have to come to me now. Best friends didn't keep secrets from each other. I could be stubborn, too.

I shuffled away from the phone, up the stairs toward my room, but didn't make it to the top. I turned around and came bounding down two steps at a time and grabbed the receiver, my trembling fingers making it very hard to dial.

I had to apologize. No matter what. Felicia surely had an incredibly good reason. Friends have to be trusted. "Hello? Felicia?" My heart was thumping loudly. "It's me."

Hearing her sigh of relief, I was so glad I'd called right back. "Listen, I'm sorry. I didn't mean what I said."

"It's okay," Felicia said. I heard a sniffle. Was she crying? Tough Felicia. F-E-A-R! I felt awful.

"Wait, while I get a tissue." Felicia blew her nose. "You know, Asa, you really didn't have to call me back."

"I didn't?"

"No. You could have communicated the way Queen Asa and your ancestors did."

"*What?*"

"Yeah. You could have used Norse Code."

"Oh!" I moaned with joy. "Felicia Esperanza Aurora Rodriguez! At last, *you* made a pun!"

"Yeah! I caught the word disease I guess. Wait till I try alliteration." She cracked up, and amid the laughing I could hear a sob or two.

Our friendship was intact.

We put the phones down long enough to check our refrigerators and decide on ham for tomorrow's sandwiches. Raw carrots to nibble on. Apple juice was the drink of choice.

"We'll eat in the schoolyard if it's a nice day," Felicia proposed. "That way we can watch the basketball game."

Basketball game? She meant the two Tarheels and Ramon horsing around.

Three more telephone consultations plus an exhaustive search of my closet and my dresser drawers fi-

nally provided an adequate — though not remarkable —
outfit. I was content. I got into my *Batgirl* sleepshirt
and climbed into bed though I knew I wouldn't sleep
a wink. Tomorrow is the moment of truth for me and
the Tarheel, I thought. How can I lie awake for so
many hours?

That was my last thought. I promptly fell fast asleep.

I looked pretty but not too dressed-up in my light tan
Chinos with a glacier green T-shirt and tan socks.

Felicia had agreed it was the perfect combination;
flattering but not hit-you-on-the-head obvious.

"You look lovely," my mother said, "like a spring
flower."

My father glanced up from the *Times* to smile at me,
and then to look at his watch. "Oh!" he said, rising in
mock alarm, "Speaking of flowers, I am a very late
poppy."

Laughing, I kissed him on the cheek, and then ate
my breakfast.

Though I started out earlier than usual and it was a
lovely morning — the sun was shining and there was a
gentle breeze lifting my hair — I didn't dawdle.

I sailed quickly down the street, heading for the Rodriguez house, so in almost no time I was standing on

the soft, hemp *Bienvenida* mat and ringing the bell. Mrs. Rodriguez opened the door before the second ring.

She must have been in the front hallway, waiting. She was not her regular smiling self though she let me in and hugged me as usual. She looked serious. Something was definitely up.

"*Buenos días, Abuelita,*" I said.

"Good morning, Asa."

I nearly flipped. I backed off staring at her face. "You said that in English!"

Mrs. Rodriguez nodded.

"But you don't speak English!"

"Now, only for you, I speak English."

Amazed, I plumped myself down on the boot-chair. "Instant English? It's a miracle! You never could speak it before."

The grandmother shook her head. "You don't understand."

"You bet I don't."

"I know English," the old woman said softly, "but I do not use it. Till this *emergencia*. Your little brother— I thought some terrible thing happened."

I was really bewildered. "I don't understand anything," I said. "This is crazy. I've been coming here every morning and trying to speak Spanish to you because you couldn't speak English. And all the time you were fooling me. Why?"

Just then Felicia shouted from the kitchen, "Clear the track! Express coming through. Open the door."

"I am sorry, Asa," Mrs. Rodriguez said softly. "I feel like you are my own family. That is why I care so much about the baby." She opened the door.

"Make way!" Felicia came rocketing along the narrow corridor, an explosion of dark hair, blue bookbag, and white cotton sweater.

"I came to New York with two treasures," the old woman began slowly, "my Roberto and my Spanish."

"*Abuelita.*" Felicia looked at her wristwatch. "*Tarde.*"

"Felicia will explain it all to you — everything."

Felicia kissed her on her cheek. "*¿Todo?*" she asked.

"*Sí. Todo.*" her grandmother said emphatically. "You will forgive me, Asa. I know you have a good heart." She patted my arm.

We went out the door. She didn't close it at once, as was her everyday habit. Instead, she lingered in the doorway watching us, and when we looked back, she waved.

We both waved back.

"I can't believe this," I said, as we started along the sun-bright street. "She speaks English! You're my best friend and you kept it a secret."

"It wasn't *my* secret," Felicia said. "It was hers."

"Why did she need to keep it such a big secret?"

"She didn't think it was anyone else's business."

"But why? She speaks very well."

"She never wanted to learn English. She was forced to."

"This is crazier and crazier. *Who* forced her?"

"It's a long story."

"Tell me. She told you to tell me *todo.*"

"Okay. When *Abuelita* came here from Puerto Rico with my father, he was just about our age. She registered him for school, but he hated it. He got into trouble every day: fights, cutting, hanging out. In June, at the end of sixth grade, they wanted to hold him back another year.

"The teacher sent for her. His name was Mr. Butler, and *Abuelita* says he spoke the worst Spanish she ever heard. His pronunciation hurt her ears, and *he* was the teacher who taught Spanish! She couldn't believe it.

"Mr. Butler told her, 'Your Roberto has failed everything. He must repeat sixth grade.'

"'No, he is a smart boy,' *Abuelita* insisted. 'He was first in his class in San Juan. He won the school prize in reading.'

"'*El no puede aprender—*' The teacher went on to explain that because Roberto did not speak or understand English, he hated school. He felt left out and needed help.

"*Abuelita* insisted it was the school's job, the teacher's job, to help him. She operated a sewing machine ten hours a day in a factory making dresses. She felt she couldn't teach him.

"'The school can't do it all alone,' the teacher told her. 'He needs to speak English outside. With friends. Most of all, at home. With family. With you.'

"'We speak Spanish at home,' *Abuelita* told him proudly. 'Like our fathers and our grandfathers.'

"'Then Roberto will fail. He must repeat sixth grade.' Mr. Butler got up. The conference was finished.

"'Wait! Roberto must not fail. It will hurt him to repeat the grade. He is large for his age. It will make him feel bad to be with small children.'

"'So?'"

"'If I must—I will allow English in the house. I will try to learn and speak with him at home. I will help him with his lessons. I will do all a mother can. You must not make him repeat the grade.' *Abuelita* was desperate.

"'Fine. There are free evening classes at the high school.'

"'I know about those classes. I will go. And I will speak English with Roberto.'

"*Abuelita* was heartbroken. She felt she would lose

her culture. But what could she do? My father had to go to school. It was life or death! School was life. The streets of the *barrio* were death.

"'But make no mistake,' she told that teacher. 'Once Roberto is safe, I will not speak English. Spanish is my language, the queen of all languages. I will not let my family become *Nuyoricanos*. Never!'

"That was what she swore that day," Felicia said, "and she kept her promise. She's very smart. She learned to speak and to read and write. She was strict with my father. She checked his homework every single night.

"He went on until he graduated from high school. After she hung his diploma on the wall, she never spoke English again. That's why I'm fluent in Spanish. We don't speak anything else to each other."

"But your father speaks English."

"Not in the house. He respects her. Though he tries to tell her the teacher was right. We should use both languages."

"All this time, you knew she could?"

Felicia nodded. "It was *her* secret."

"Telephoning my mother must have been a major case for her," I said, awed.

"You're my best friend, and she cares a lot about you. That's how she is. When I came home and told her how you left school with your father because there was an emergency, she was frightened. She was sure it was the baby. Then when you didn't show up or call yesterday morning, she got really frantic. But I didn't know she phoned your mother till you told me. You believe me, don't you?"

"Of course. It's all so complicated. I mean—here's your grandmother who hardly goes out of the house and she has this tremendous secret . . ." I stopped, overwhelmed by the morning's events.

"You know, Asa, many times when you were *muy biening* all over the place, I wanted to tell you but I just couldn't."

"What a story!" I marveled. "Who would have thought your little old grandma was so tough? Will she speak to me in English after this? I mean, now that I know."

"Probably not. She wants you to learn Spanish, the queen of all languages."

I nodded. *"Muy bien."*

"But she might speak English to your mother. She loved talking to her about the baby."

"My mother would love that, too. It's her favorite subject."

I slipped into my seat, my eyes averted so I didn't have to look at the Tarheel. I felt terrific tension. There was no point in pretending nothing had happened, so

I decided to be bold and take matters into my own hands.

I wrote him a note:

Thank you for sending the baseball card to my brother.

Writing was so much easier than speaking. I put my hand up behind my back and dropped the scrap of paper onto his desk. As my father would say (and Julius Caesar before him), the die was cast.

No answer came.

All morning as I did my assignments, I kept one eye out for a scrap, a tiny folded sheet, anything.

The hours passed and no message came. Absolutely nothing happened. I was disappointed and suddenly very shy. I would have liked to disappear.

Lunch hour, Felicia and I went out into the schoolyard and sat on our favorite bench. We ate our ham sandwiches and drank our apple juice, admiring the tiny crocuses coming up in the small flower bed nearby. It was really spring, at last.

For about fifteen minutes, we had the place completely to ourselves and it was unbelievably quiet. Most of the kids stayed in the crowded lunchroom; that was where the action was.

Then, a while after we'd finished eating, we heard the door bang open and the sound of a basketball thumping on the pavement. The boys were coming outside at last.

The three basketballers came running along, dribbling the ball, tossing it one to the other, and generally fooling around as they leaped and pushed and tried to score impossible baskets.

They knew they were being watched. They were playing for the fun of it, but they were also performing for their audience.

One thing was certain: nothing could happen out here. There could not possibly be a conversation during basketball.

I would have to spend the whole afternoon session, again sitting in front of him, rigid and nervous, pretending that I was invisible or he was invisible or we both just weren't there.

Let him talk to me, I wished fervently. Let him just say something. Let us straighten things out so the end of sixth grade will be a pleasure.

He doesn't have to like me. Just so he doesn't hate me any more. I can't sit there in front of him like a big stupid dodo bird without feelings.

Concentrating on these wishes totally, I was startled when Ramon suddenly cupped his hand over his mouth to yell at us from way over where he stood.

"F-Felicia," he called, "w-want to play?"

"Do I ever!" Felicia murmured, and, in a second, the white cardigan was on the bench and she was up and on her way to the basketball court.

She looked very small hurrying out there, petite and remarkably pretty, her curly hair flying in the breeze and her eyes bright with excitement.

By the time she arrived under the basket, the three had become two: only Ramon and Tommy Lee were waiting there for her.

He was walking carefully along the white boundary line on the edge of the court, his head down, concentrating like a circus high-wire acrobat on staying on the line.

He was headed toward the bench where I sat. I suddenly got very busy picking lint from my chinos as I saw him approaching. I watched his progress but not directly.

Now his two big feet stood in front of me.

"Hey there," he said.

I looked up, shading my eyes against the sun. "You talking to me?"

He looked at the empty bench on both sides of me. "Mmm."

I waited.

"There's something I have to say."

I was silent. For a long time, nothing was forthcoming. "Go ahead," I said finally. "Say it."

He just stood there digging at the cement with his heel.

"Well?" I said.

"If you could just stay quiet and be a little patient, I'm working out how to say it," he sighed. "New Yorkers are all in such a big hurry."

I was silent now with astonishment. Nothing happened. Lunch hour would end any minute. The world could end any minute. He would still be working out what to say.

I tried to help him start. "It was nice of you to send the card."

"That's cool. I'm glad your little brother is getting better."

"My father said the card looks expensive. We'll get it back to you when the baby comes home."

"No. It's a real present for the baby."

I nodded. I resumed the hunt for lint on my pants.

The heel continued to dig at the pavement. "It's not so expensive. Tell your father. It's not an original, but it is a very good card. It's from the 1962 Topps Series."

Again, I nodded.

"It's real hard for me to get this out, to say this, but I'm sorry I called you—" he choked on the word "—Fatso. 'Cause I think you're real pretty."

I had helped him start, but now he was on his own and doing mighty well.

"I didn't mean any harm. I was just mad 'cause you tripped me."

"I accept your apology."

"I'm not done." He stopped again. "You see, your true name—Asa—well, it just struck me as strange because of my uncle. Uncle Asa is six foot four and he's a champion lightweight boxer."

Uh, uh, I thought. Here we go again.

"Anyway, back home it wouldn't 've mattered," he explained. "The teasing, I mean. It's just a way I joke with girls. They never minded."

"I mind."

"I know." He stopped talking, but his foot kept scuffing the sidewalk. "Never again. I promise."

I shaded my eyes again so I could look up.

From the basketball court came screams of triumph. "I did it. I did it!"

Felicia was jumping around madly. Tommy Lee stood there open-mouthed as if he'd just witnessed a miracle.

"Michael Jordan, watch out," Ramon shouted. "P-Patrick Ewing take care!"

"You said I should never say your name. Would you? Do you think? Can I?" He started three different sentences, but he couldn't finish a single one. His voice broke. This was almost too much for him. He struggled on, manfully.

"I mean, you sit right in front of me. We should be friends. Since we're in the same class and all."

I took my time, so it would look like I was thinking it over. "Sure," I said, finally. "No hard feelings."

Again, I let several beats go by, then with courage I didn't know I had, I took a terrible chance. "If we're going to be real friends, you might as well know I have a weirder middle name. It's Alfifa."

"Say what?" He stopped kicking the pavement.

"Alfifa." I spelled it. "She was another queen."

He looked at me sympathetically. "I guess there's nothing you can do about it. If I were you, I wouldn't go around telling folks."

"I don't. Only Felicia knows, and now you."

He smiled. "Want to go one on one, Asa?" He tilted his head toward the basketball court.

"No. That's what we've been doing ever since you came to this school. Let's just go shoot baskets with the others."

"*All right!*" As he put his hand out to pull me up off the bench, he was struck by an odd thought. "Say, do you think Uncle Asa knows he's named for a queen?"

"I doubt it. But if I were you, I wouldn't mention it to him. Anyway, Asa is a unisex name."

He grinned. "Way to go. Race you to the basket."

We headed onto the court running side-by-side, the boys cheering for him and Felicia for me.

It didn't matter who won.